SANDWICH

SANDWICH

A Novel

CATHERINE NEWMAN

HARPER

An Imprint of HarperCollinsPublishers

HarperCollins books may be purchased for educational, business, or sales promotional use. For information, please email the Special Markets Department at SPsales@harpercollins.com.

FIRST EDITION

Designed by Nancy Singer

Library of Congress Cataloging-in-Publication Data has been applied for.

ISBN 978-0-06-334516-4

24 25 26 27 28 LBC 5 4 3 2 1

This one is for my parents, whom I love so immoderately.

SANDWICH

Prologue

Picture this: a shorelined peninsula jutting into the Atlantic Ocean. Zoom in a little closer. It's a Cape Cod beach town. It's midsummer. The narrow highway is thick with lobster dinners and mini-golf windmills and inflatable bagel pool floats. But turn off the main drag in either direction and find yourself quickly at the sea: sandy cliffs and windswept grasses; tumbling pink roses and vast blue skies and a tideline hemmed with stones and mussels and bright green ruffles of seaweed. Beneath the waves: shivers of great white sharks, stuffed to the gills—or so one imagines—with surfers.

In the passenger seat of one slightly rusting silver Subaru station wagon: a woman in her fifties. She is halfway in age between her young adult children and her elderly parents. She is long married to a beautiful man who understands between twenty and sixty-five percent of everything she says. Her body is a wonderland. Or maybe her body is a satchel full of scars and secrets and menopause. They've been coming here for so many years that there's a watercolor wash over all of it now: Everything hard has been smeared out into pleasant, pastel memories of taffy, clam strips, and beachcombing. Sunglasses and sunscreen and sandy feet pressed against her thighs and stomach. Little children running across the sand with their little pails. Her own parents laughing in their beach chairs, shrinking inside their clothes as the years pass. Grief bright in the periphery, like a light flashing just out of view.

The woman and her husband have fetched the grown children from the train station. They're headed to the small house they rent for this one week every year. She's so happy to have the kids with her that she doesn't know what to do with herself besides crane around to look at them and smile. It's the one moment of the trip when she won't complain about the traffic.

"And we are put on earth a little space, that we may learn to bear the beams of love," she says, unprompted.

"Is that a poem?" her twenty-year-old daughter asks. It is.

"Who?" the daughter asks.

"William Blake."

"What's it called?"

The woman grimaces. "I think it might be called 'The Little Black Boy.'"

"Ugh, Mom!"

"I know, I know. But I think it's okay?"

"I seriously doubt it."

"I think he was an abolitionist?"

"One of the abolitionists who kept enslaved people?"

"Good question," the mother says.

"Is it beams like wood?" the daughter asks. "Or beams like light in your eyes?"

"I don't know." She has always pictured it both ways: squinting against the unbearable lightness of loving while simultaneously crouched under the heavy cross of it. "It's so crushingly beautiful, being human," the mother sighs, and the daughter rolls her eyes and says, "But also so terrible and ridiculous."

And maybe it's all three.

This one week.

SATURDAY

1

"Oh my god! Oh my god! Oh my god!" I'm laughing. I'm screaming and also crying. The water is rising, rising, rising up to the rim of the toilet. "Nick! Nick! Nicky!" Yelling is my only contribution to this situation, it seems. My husband has the plunger in his hands but he's watching the water as if in a trance. In a cartoon, the swirl in the bowl would be mirrored in his hypnotized eyes. "Nicky! Nick!"

Nick appears to come to. He bends over the toilet, twists something near the floor, and there's a clanking sound, a gasp from the pipes. The water stills. "Jesus," I say. "Phew."

Then something appears in the toilet. Something like a large silver jellyfish. What even is that? An air bubble? A giant air bubble! It pushes the contents of the toilet bowl up and over, all of it sloshing onto the floor like a waterfall. A waterfall, if a waterfall were inside the house and had disintegrating toilet paper in it and worse. I leap up onto the edge of the tub, the better to hear myself screaming, it would seem.

"How bad is it in there?" Our daughter is yelling through the closed door. "Oh my god, you guys, ew! Tell me how bad it is! I can smell it! It stinks! It smells like used radishes out here."

"Honey, it's fine! We've got it," Nick yells. He's bent over the toilet with the plunger again, working it like he's churning some kind of debased butter.

"Your dad is lying!" I call out to Willa. "We're, like, knee-deep in sewage."

Nick looks up at me and smiles. "Are we *knee-deep in sewage*, Rocky?"

We are not.

"We are," I say. "I like how that T-shirt fits you, actually," I add. "Just as a side note." He laughs, flexes his sexy biceps. There's a sudden sucking sound, and the rest of the water swirls away. Nick bends over again calmly and twists the valve to refill the bowl.

We're at the cottage—the same one we've been renting every summer for twenty years. It's late afternoon on Saturday. We've been here for approximately one hour. Less, maybe. We know better than to overwhelm this ancient septic system—there's even a framed calligraphy admonition hanging over the toilet that says, DO NOT OVERWHELM THE ANCIENT SEPTIC SYSTEM!—but, well, here we are.

"Do you need help?" Willa calls in. "Say no, though. I actually really don't want to help. Jamie needs to know the Wi-Fi password."

"I think it's still *chowder123*, all lowercase," I say.

"Thanks," she says. We hear her call it out to her brother. "Sorry, also, do you guys know where the bag is with the swimsuits in it?"

"Fuck," Nick says. He straightens up. "Did you already look in the car?" he calls out to Willa, and she says, "Yeah."

"Fuck," Nick says again. "I'm worried I may have left it in the hallway at home. I can kind of picture it there."

"Are you kidding me?" I say. I'm still standing on the edge of the tub, balancing myself with a hand on the shower-curtain rod. "I specifically said, 'Did you get all the bags out of the hallway?' And you were like, 'Yeah, yeah, I got all the bags.'"

"Right," he says. "I know. I guess I didn't." He doesn't look at me when he says this. "It's not, like, a massive crisis. We can get new swimsuits in town."

"Okay," I say. "But you totally minimized my concern about *whether we had all the fucking bags*." Ugh, my voice! You can actually hear the estrogen plummeting inside my larynx.

"Jesus, Rocky." He's dragging a bath towel around the floor with his foot now. "It's not a big deal."

"I didn't say it was a big deal," I say quietly, but my veins are flooded with the lava that's spewing out of my bad-mood volcano. If menopause were an actual substance, it would be spraying from my eyeballs, searing the word *ugh* across Nick's cute face. "Just acknowledge that you never really listen to me when I ask you something."

"Never," he says flatly. "Wow. Good to know."

"Are you guys standing around in shit water and fighting?" Willa calls in. "Are you having a meta fight about the way you're fighting? Don't. Dad, did you apologize for whatever it is that Mama's mad about? You should probably just apologize and get on with your life."

"I did," he says, and I roll my eyes. "Did you, though?" I say, and he shrugs, says, "Close enough."

"Willa," I call out. "We're good. We've got this. Go do something else for a few minutes."

"Okay—but ew, something's seeping out from under the door. Oh, okay, Jamie's saying it's *chowder* with a capital *C*. Ew, you guys! Clean up in there and then come out," Willa calls. "I want to figure out the swimsuit situation."

"Yes," I say. "We will." And then there's a popping sound, which, it turns out, is the sound of the curtain rod unsuctioning itself from the wall. 1 lose my balance, grab at the slippery starfish-printed fabric that is no longer attached to anything, and splat onto the floor, banging my head on the edge of the sink and thwacking Nick in the face with the rod. I'm on my back, the shower curtain twisted over my body like a shroud.

Nick looks down at me, not overly alarmed. "How's your vacation going so far?" he says, and smiles. Then he reaches down with both hands to help me up.

2

"Don't mind my parents," Willa is saying to the young woman who works at the surf shop. "They had an accident in the bathroom."

I'm limping—there's something in one of my knees that feels like a crumbling old rubber band—and Nick has the beginning of a black eye, the area beneath his dark lashes turning swollen and plummy. Back in the cottage, the bathroom is clean, and, in the little laundry building of the complex, the towels are running in a very hot wash with a big slug of bleach. Nick and I have showered, and we've also inspected each other's wounds mockingly, which is going to have to count as making up.

"I'm sorry," I whisper to Willa. "Are you using Plungergate as an excuse to flirt with the cute girl?"

"So?" she says, and laughs, winks at me. When I look over a minute later, the cute girl is typing something into Willa's phone.

I wanted to drive to the Ocean State Job Lot—the discount place—to look for scratch-and-dent suits, but I got voted off that particular island. So here we are.

We've spent no small fraction of our lives in this shop. When you think of Cape Cod, you might picture those lapis skies or skies tiered in glorious bands of gray. You might picture the wild stretches of beach backed by rugged dunes or quaintly shingled houses with clouds of blue hydrangea blossoming all over the place. You might think of the deep steel blue of the sea as the setting sun puddles into it in melting popsicle colors. Which is funny, because most of the time you're actually at the surf shop or the weird little supermarket that smells like raw meat, or in line at the clam shack, the good bakery, the port-a-potty, the mini-golf place. You're buying twenty-dollar sunscreen at the gas station. You're waiting for your child to pick out six pieces of saltwater taffy with the beach in a querying thought bubble above your head while your beard turns white and grows down to the floor, pages flying off the calendar. You're waiting at the walk-in clinic because the kids have sudden fevers and, it turns out, strep throat; you're waiting at the old-fashioned pharmacy for the ancient pharmacist to mix up—or maybe *invent*—the antibiotics that will make everyone need to lean out from their narrow beds with the anchor-printed coverlets and barf fever-ishly into the speckled enamel lobster pot you've placed on the floor between them. But also, yes, beaches and ponds and epic skies. All of it.

"I think I'm just getting these again." Jamie is holding out a pair of black board shorts in the hand his girlfriend, Maya, isn't holding.

"Great," I say. "I'm really glad you packed your own swim-suit," I say to Maya. "Feel free to get something if you want, though!"

"I'm good," she says, "but thank you."

Maya, like Jamie and Willa and young people everywhere,

is a perfect human specimen. Her hair cascades—it actually *cascades!*—over her shoulders in shiny black curls in a way that makes me reach back to feel my own damp ponytail, as narrow as your grandma's crochet hook. Her skin glows and gleams. She's got a pair of tiny silver hoops in one perfect nostril and a pair of enormous silver hoops in her two perfect ears. She's wearing just the merest suggestion of cutoffs and also a garment that is, I think, a bra—but which I'm told is a *bralette*, which means it is a shirt. I am here for all of it—the young people and their bodies. I wish I'd dressed like that when I was their age instead of in the burlap sack dresses we favored for their astonishing shapelessness. "What's in there?" people surely wondered. *A youthful human torso and legs? A truckload of Idaho potatoes?* There was no telling.

"I'm glad you're here," I say, smiling at Maya, and she says, "Me too."

"I'm just going to get these same ones I got last year." Nick is holding out a pair of black board shorts that is either similar or identical to Jamie's. Willa's getting a gray sports bra and the same shorts as her father and older brother.

"Okay, okay," I say. "Shit. You guys are fast. I've got to try some stuff on. I don't even know what size I am this year." I look down as if the top view of my boobs is going to resolve into a numeral. "Help me. I need something with, I don't know, some kind of padding? Some kind of *compression* something or other."

"Just get one that's comfortable, Mama," Willa says. "Or you're going to be picking it out of your ass crack and mad at Dad the whole time about forgetting the swimsuits." This is probably true. I run my hands over the rack of one-pieces and

I am suddenly remembering buying a suit here twenty years ago, when Jamie was three and I was very pregnant with Willa. My boobs were enormous again. When I'd gone to put on the tankini I'd worn through multiple summers of pregnancy and nursing, the taxed elastic had made that sad ripping sound, the one that means it won't be snapping back again after. Come to think of it, I'm surprised my actual body doesn't make that sound every time I bend over.

"What?" Willa says. She's looking at my face. "What's going on with you, besides being concussed or whatever you are?"

How are you an adult? is one question I don't ask. *Are all those little girls nested inside you like matryoshka dolls?* is another. All those summers of the kids with their sticky hands and sticky faces and excitedness! "Just sentimental," I say instead, and kiss her perfect rosy empath cheek. I try on two different sizes of the same navy-blue tank suit. ("Keep your underpants on!" Willa yells helpfully into the fitting room because when we were her age we probably went nudely into the changing cabinet to infect all the woolen swim costumes with syphilis.) The suit that doesn't squinch my groin is gappy at the chest. I jog in place and it's not good. One big wave and my boobs will definitely be celebrating their dangly freedom. The one that's snugger, though, feels like it's going to pinch my legs all the way off. It also bisects my butt in a way that makes it look like I have two distinct sets of ass cheeks. The more the merrier! But actually less merry. There is also some kind of situation between my rib cage and legs—something new that looks like a bag full of dinner rolls. Or maybe just a large loaf of peasant bread.

YOU ARE ON UNCEDED WAMPANOAG TERRITORY, someone has written on the door in Sharpie. My aging body is not going to change the course of history one way or another. I pick the roomier suit.

"That was a fun two hundred dollars to spend!" I say in the car, and everyone grumbles at me to let it go.

"Check your privilege," Willa says, and I can't tell if she's teasing or not—but she's right.

"That's fair," I say. "Is it *check* like check it at the door? Or *check* like take a good hard look?"

"I don't know," Willa says. "Just pick one and do it."

"Beach?" Nick says. "Dinner? What's everyone feeling like?" What everyone is feeling like is quick beach and then clam shack. Nick signals to turn toward the bay.

"Wait," I say, craning around to talk to Jamie. "Did you tell Daddy about your work—the nice thing your supervisor said?"

"Ew, Mom," Willa says.

"What?"

"Don't call him Daddy."

"Oh, right," I say. "I forgot that we're not supposed to say *daddy*. Even in the car, when it's just us. We might think we're sex trafficking each other!"

"Do you guys even know what *daddy* means?"

"Yes, Willa. We know what *daddy* means." Do we, though? I'm not actually sure. I mean, I'm the same person who thought the Fleetwood Mac song "Oh, Daddy" was about Stevie Nicks's father, to whom she seemed to be unusually devoted. Nick looks at me quickly and grimaces, shrugs.

"Okay, then, tell your peepaw," I say to Jamie, who laughs and says, "I think I'll just tell him later."

When we get down to the water's edge, the sun is disappearing behind pink-and-blue cotton-candy clouds. The sand is damp and cool, freckled with dark stones and white bits of shell. There are only a handful of other people, everyone turned toward the horizon. We hold up towels so that Nick and Willa can take turns changing into their new suits, both of them tearing off tags in a way that makes me cringe. *Don't rip the fabric!* I don't say, because, duh. The rest of us watch from the shore as they run screaming together through the froth. I see Willa wrap her arms around his neck so that Nick can bounce her in the waves like a baby. *Daddy*, I think, because I'm stubborn. Because he's been their daddy so long, his strong arms holding them in the water and out of it. Holding me too. It's hard to change, even though, I know, I know. You have to change.

I remember standing here with Jamie when he was four. I was pregnant and he was afraid of the water. I had to squat down so he could wrap his fretful little arm around my head. "Daddy is okay," he said, like a mantra, pointing at the speck of his father's head. "Daddy is a good swimmer and is okay." I rubbed his little velvet shoulder. "Daddy's fine," I said. "He's having a lovely time in the water. You'll join him again out there when you feel like it." I was so tired. "I will," he said thoughtfully. "I would like to." The following summer I watched from the beach while Jamie bobbed in the waves with his dad.

I shake my head now. Willa and Nick are clambering back toward us through the wavelets, the sun just a sliver of color tracing the water behind them. "Sunrise, sunset," I sing out, and Willa sings with me: "Swiftly fly the years! One season following another—laden with happiness and tears."

"And claaaaaams!" Willa yells. "Oh my god, I'm starving!" And suddenly, I realize, so am I.

3

Willa's mad at the candy store. Specifically, she's mad at Jamie, who has simply purchased a half pound of rocky-road fudge rather than spending an hour with her studying the penny candy like there's an exam coming up and one question will be a compare and contrast about flying-saucer Satellite Wafers versus Zotz.

"Take your time," Jamie says to her from the bench on the store's front porch, where he and Maya are sitting under the twinkle lights and licking fudge off their fingers. Nick and I are on the other bench, sharing a bag of chocolate-covered pretzels even though I'm as stuffed with seafood as a seal. "We're not in a rush."

"That's not the point," Willa says. She's standing in the doorway holding a little basket that currently contains two individual Swedish Fish and a Blow Pop. "Jamie, you can't just leave me to do all my baby things by myself. It's too sad."

This candy store! The kids used to vibrate with excitement if you even mentioned it. It's almost painful, the way little children just trustingly hold out their hearts for you to look at—the way they haven't learned yet how to conceal what matters to them, even if it's just chewing gum or a plush dolphin or plastic binoculars.

Jamie stands. "Can I please have a dollar, Dad?" he says, and Nick fishes one out of his wallet. "Let's see what they've got this year!" he says, joining Willa in the store, and she says, "You're the best."

"Maya, you can have a dollar too!" I say, and she laughs, says she's good.

"Were they always like this?" she says.

"Willa and Jamie?" She nods. "I think the answer is yes. But I probably should ask what you mean," I say.

"Mmmm." She's thinking, leaning forward now over her golden legs and gleaming like a doubloon. "Like, were they always easy?"

"Ah," I say. "I think they were. I mean, that wasn't always our experience of raising them." I look at Nick, who smiles reflexively, but I think he's just eating pretzels and spacing out. "Actually, it was probably Nick's experience of raising them. But I sometimes felt kind of overwhelmed by everybody's feelings and rashes and whatever." Hello, understatement! "And, I mean, sometimes they bickered or were mad at me or sad about the idea of the summer ending. Jamie always cried when the first back-to-school circulars arrived. But, yeah, they were always more or less the way they are."

"That must have been so fun," she says. "When they were babies. I mean, I've seen some of the pictures."

"It was fun," I say. In my memory, they roll through the world like delighted beach balls. Also, they lie on top of me in a damply sobbing tangle of miserable arms and legs. I feel like there's something Maya wants to hear or say, but I'm not sure what it is. "Was it fun for you, being a little kid?"

She waves the question away with her hand. "Not really. There were so many of us," she says. Maya is the middle child of five. "It was kind of chaotic. Yeah, I guess it was fun too. I don't know. It wasn't so"—she hesitates—"intentional, the way you guys always seem."

"*Seem* might be the operative word in that sentence," I say, and she smiles. "Also I'm guessing *intentional* is a polite word for *overly precious*. But yeah."

"Did you ever want more kids than just the two?"

"No," I lie. "Two was perfect. What about you? Do you picture having kids?"

"Oh my god, Mom." Jamie is suddenly standing in the doorway with his little candy basket. "Sorry, Maya. She's the worst."

"It's okay," Maya says to him. "Yes, definitely," she says to me.

No time soon, I hope! I don't say, even though that's my next line in the sitcom script. But you really never know what you're dealing with, do you?

Besides, we're interrupted by Willa calling to us from inside the store. The candy necklace has pushed her over the dollar limit and she needs more money.

More! It was Jamie's first word. It's the call of children everywhere. And it's how I feel about my time with them now. About parenting in general, maybe, now that the days of oversaturation are long behind us. *More, more, more!*

SUNDAY

4

Nick and I are in line at the good bakery, fighting quietly in the blazing sun.

"You're actually mad at me because I couldn't predict which breakfast pastry you'd choose?"

This is technically true. "No," I say. I sigh. "I just feel so"— what?—"*unknown* by you."

"Because I thought you'd get a cherry-cheese Danish?"

"Because I never get sweet things in the morning. We've been together almost thirty years, Nicky. Have I one time gotten something sweet in the morning?"

"You got almond croissants when we went to Paris," he says. This is also true.

"Except for that."

He sighs. "I don't know, Rocky. I guess not. I'm sorry I don't know you better. In the *bakery* sense." He laughs, which is annoying to me right now on an almost cellular level. The woman ahead of us turns her straw-hatted head to look at me, turns back quickly. The woman behind us says, "Move forward. You can move forward. The line is moving!" This little hydrangea-filled Puritan colonizer beach town is completely overrun with New Yorkers.

We inch forward just enough to get under the building's overhang, and the sudden shade rearranges my mood. Can I not simply order a cheddar-chive scone without, as my father would say, making a federal case out of it? "I'm sorry," I say. "Ignore me. I think I'm having a hot flash. And a caffeine deficit. Also maybe a hangover? I don't know. I'm sorry. I'm the worst." He wraps an arm around me and kisses the side of my sweaty head. Nick is as quick to forgive as he is slow to apologize. "You really are," he says fondly.

Forty minutes later, we are walking back to the cottage with two lattes, four chocolate croissants, one scone, three baguettes, and a receipt for sixty-five dollars.

"Can you believe we're even up?" Nick says, and I'm thinking the same thing. It used to be that the kids were awake first, dressed in their little shorts and sandals and ready to walk to the bakery before it even opened at seven. I have a memory of Jamie at four, Willa a baby in the sling, me with my permanently trashed perineum, our group moving so slowly that the four blocks unspooled into an exhausted marathon of shuffling and also pointing, alarmed, to various possible patches of poison ivy. Was that fretful child really the same Jamie who now—at least according to an Instagram photo he was tagged in—appears to favor perching on the ledge of a skyscraper the better to inhale deeply from a Venetian glass bong? The same bright-eyed little Jamie who will sleep into the afternoon every day this week? They all will. "Wake me at two tomorrow," Willa had said when I was going to bed last night. "I don't want to miss anything!"

"What do you want to do this morning?" Nick asks affably

over our breakfast on the splintery little deck of the cottage. "Beach? Pond? Run? Bike?" Even though they're fleetingly with us this week, we've become accustomed to organizing ourselves around the periphery of the hole the kids have left behind. Jamie lives in New York, working some kind of marketing or engineering job at a tech start-up, and Willa just finished her junior year at Barnard. It's so new, the emptied nest, that Nick and I still make occasionally nervous small talk over our early dinners, as if we're on an awkward zillionth date at a retirement home. "The chicken is a little dry but tasty," I've heard myself say more than once.

"Hmmm," I say now. I'm punching the word C-U-N-T-Y into the Spelling Bee, just to entertain myself. *Not in word list*, the Bee responds, deadpan. I see *T-E-A-T* but refuse to enter it. What am I—a sow nursing her piglets? "I'm lazy. Let's drink our coffee and then make more coffee and then maybe go to the beach?"

"Perfect," Nick says. He's doing something on his phone too, squinting in the sunshine. "Scrabble?" I say, and he nods. "Luca?" He nods again. Luca is my college boyfriend. Asha, Nick's other favorite competitor, is my friend who hasn't spoken to me in twenty years—since she accused me of disliking her husband, which I did. "Do you play with anyone who isn't a weird ex of mine?" I ask him, and he says, "Debbie," which makes me laugh. Debbie is Nick's high school girlfriend. This particular collection of friendly competitors might be Nick in a nutshell. When we were first sleeping together as college students, I couldn't believe my good luck in finding someone with such an absolute absence of jealousy. "Have fun!" he'd say pleasantly when I was meeting an old boyfriend for drinks. On the other hand, I worried that his niceness was kind of boring. Now that niceness—that gentle impulse to say yes to everything— has become the very foundation of my entire life. Although would I mind a sexy little flash of possessiveness every now and then? Probably, yeah, I would.

In the tiny kitchen, beneath the spiral staircase that leads up to the open loft where Nick and I sleep, I find that the vintage white Mr. Coffee has been replaced with a candy-apple-red Nespresso machine. This is obviously an upgrade, beverage-wise. But I'm a little sad. That old machine, with its yellowed plastic! I have been in a nearly romantic relationship with it. I'm opening the pine cabinets now, looking for coffee capsules, closing each one quietly, since Willa's asleep on the sofa bed that's about five feet away from me. Every cabinet exhales its familiar smell of Old Bay seasoning and something else, which is probably—when I stop to think about it—mice.

This is not an upscale rental. When Nick first found it on-line, he read the description aloud to me. "It looks nice," he said. "Yeah," I said, "but *architect designed*? Shouldn't that kind of go without saying? It's like their main brag about the house—that it wasn't designed by accountants or surfers." Still, the cottage was so much cheaper than anything else we'd seen—one of a cluster of pretty little cedar-shingled houses. As was the custom with the old Cape rentals, you had to bring your own sheets and towels. You still do.

Aha! The capsules are in the drawer with the foil and the sandwich bags and the clothespins and the take-out packets of ketchup and soy sauce and a candle stub and three dice. I'm pressing the START button on the machine when Maya flies out of the bedroom and sprints into the bathroom, slamming the door behind her. Willa sits up in bed, wide-eyed. "Yikes!" I say, and Willa grimaces. Maya is either coughing in a noisy, gagging way or, more likely, throwing up. If a stomach bug rips through the cottage, I will saw my own head off with this dull bread knife.

"Oh my god," I say to Willa. "I can't believe this is happening again."

"Again?" she says. "Oh, you mean, *again* since it happened that one summer when I was, like, four?"

"Yeah," I say sheepishly. "I hadn't really realized it was so long ago."

"Poor Maya," Willa says, and I say, "Yes. I meant *poor Maya*!"

We hear the toilet successfully flushing (praise god), the water running in the sink, and Maya emerges, her face pale.

I put an arm around her lovely shoulders, push the damp curls off her face. "You poor thing," I say. "Do you think you might be pregnant?"

Willa is wide-eyed with horror. "Oh my god, Mom! Can you please not? I'm sorry, Maya. She has, like, zero boundaries. As you know."

"Not pregnant," Maya says, and laughs, knocks her knuckles on the wooden door frame. "Maybe something I ate last night? There was definitely a clam that didn't taste so great."

"Can you tell if you feel better or worse now?"

"Definitely better," she says. She bends down to heft up Chicken, our massive old tabby cat, then climbs into bed next to Willa. I decide not to be the germaphobe bullfrog that I am, croaking out my frog song about microbes and contagion, and instead pour her a glass of icy seltzer. Nick comes in through the sliding door just as his coffee is done brewing.

"We've got a barfing going on in here," I say, and he looks over sympathetically at the girls, who are sitting up in bed, Chicken sprawled on his back across their laps. Willa points to Maya. Nick frowns, nods, takes the mug I'm handing him, and sits at the little round table that's wedged under the staircase.

Jamie emerges rumpledly from the bedroom, squeezes onto the sofa bed. "You okay, honey?" he says, and Maya shrugs, smiles, says, "Fine, I think."

"Did my mom already ask if you were pregnant?" he says, and she nods. "Classic," he says, and shakes his head. I tear off a piece of baguette and hold it up questioningly. Maya reaches out her hand.

Because, remarkably, everybody's up, we decide we'll all head to the beach. But first: the epic making of the sandwiches! I complain about this part of my vacation life, but I love it, and everybody knows this. I look for my favorite bowl—the one with the Scandinavian mushrooms printed around its enamel sides—and mix three cans of tuna with half a jar of mayo, heaps of celery, pickled pepperoncini peppers, and a splash of juice from the pepper jar. Jamie, Nick, and I all want fresh dill and cucumbers in our sandwiches. Nick also wants honey mustard, lettuce, basil, and tomatoes, even though I judge him about the chaotic too-muchness of it. Willa, a clam-eating vegetarian, wants a mozzarella and roasted pepper sandwich, which Maya wants too—though she's not totally sure if she'll eat it. Willa wants fresh basil on hers and a drizzle of balsamic; Maya wants only cucumbers.

I complain joyfully about how particular everyone is, wrap

everything in foil, stick it all in the cooler, add a package of Vienna Fingers cookies, a big bag of cherries, dill-pickle potato chips, a half-dozen cans of lemon-lime seltzer, a big mason jar full of water with lemon slices in it, and a couple cans of beer. We disappear into various rooms to clamber into swimsuits and then some of us put on sunscreen (me, Willa), while others of us claim they'll put it on at the beach.

"Hopefully I'll be dead by the time you get skin cancer," I say to Jamie, and he says, "Nice, Mom," but doesn't actually look up from his phone.

Nick does my back like he's a yeti with a yeti's massive cryptid paws, getting sunscreen in my hair and all over my new suit in the process. You half expect to hear him groaning behind me like Frankenstein. "You're welcome," he says when I complain.

"Mom, you do mine," Willa says to me. "No offense, Dad."

Sometimes, if I have an excuse to touch the kids, I have to will myself to be normal. Their perfect bodies! So off-limits to me now. When they were little there was so *much* of it—the touching. Too much. Skin on skin in the bed, in the bath, on the beach. Their sticky, gritty little legs wrapped around my torso every second, their popsicle hands in my hair. I loved it. I leaned my face down to inhale their scalps and foreheads. But what I wouldn't have given to plant a flag on myself—to claim a single square inch of my own flesh. Back then, if Nick slipped his randy, sandy, sunscreeny hands along my sideboobs, I would say, like the cautionary tale in a book about marital longevity, "Are you fucking kidding me?" But now there's so much less of all of it—the grasping and the groping. I miss it.

Which I know better than to mention while I'm rubbing sunscreen into the ruddy silk of Willa's skin. She is, essentially, a human piece of fruit—a thought I keep to myself. Oops! I guess I don't! "I'm not a *nectarine*," she says irritably, like she's five. *I'm a girl. A* big *girl!* she doesn't say now.

As far as maternal duties go, putting sunscreen on the kids is about as gratifying as serving them steaming bowls of borscht for dinner. When they were little, you'd have thought we were slathering Willa and Jamie in boiling tar. They *wanted* to get skin cancer, they cried. They at least wanted the spray kind of sunscreen, which I forbade because *endocrine disruptor*. They both swore that the first thing they'd do when they turned eighteen was not wear sunscreen ever again. "Maybe *first* buy a naked-people magazine, *then* not wear sunscreen," Jamie conceded once about his robust plans for legal adulthood. I put aerosol Coppertone in their Christmas stockings last year, because I'm hilarious. "Ha ha, very funny," they said.

"Ugh, that's too much lotion," Willa complains now, craning her darkly shorn head around to narrow her brown eyes at me, her eyelashes a luxurious and irritable fringe, and I say, "Well, you're twenty, honey, so feel free to—" and she interrupts me. "Stop. Jesus. Just use less."

By the time everyone is ready it is, mysteriously, one o'clock—a phenomenon we call Cape Cod Time Warp and never understand. It is always one o'clock when we leave for the beach, regardless of when we start readying ourselves. We've got an annual sticker, so we can park at the National Seashore and take the open-air tram to the ocean. Everybody loves the tram. Sometimes, when the kids were little, we'd just stay on the tram, ride it around half the day while we chatted and snacked. "Fancy seeing you again!" one particular driver would say, to make the kids laugh. It was so relaxing—a guilty pleasure, for some reason, as if I should have preferred carrying everybody in their sodden swim diaper, crying, across the burning sand.

While we're waiting at the tram stop now, Jamie asks us if we'd give up our lives for better lives—but they'd be simulations. "You'd basically be having a virtual reality experience," he says. "But it would be really, really pleasurable." He's all sparkle, this kid. All dimples and head-cocked curiosity, his dark hair spilling over his forehead like his father's. We call him The Funcooker.

I catch Maya's eye and she mouths, *He's so cute!* Neither of us is even listening to him all that attentively, but Willa is. "I don't know," she says. "Would I be gone from my real life and people would miss me?"

"Yes," Jamie says.

Willa sighs. "Then I'd definitely stay in my real life."

"Not me!" Nick says robustly. "I'd go for the fun virtual one." I swivel my head to look at him, and he backpedals. "I mean, as long as Mom didn't mind," he adds, lamely. "Not that my life isn't already perfect," he adds, also lamely.

"That makes sense," I say, "since you're basically a robot already." I'd meant this to be funnier than it ends up sounding, and the kids exchange nervous glances before Willa says, "Sick burn," and they laugh.

"It's true," Nick says affably. "The world of human feelings is not really my forte."

"Same," Jamie says, and they fist-bump. Jesus.

I would pick this life too, I know. I'd even pick the way that pain has burnished me to brightness. The pain itself, though? I imagine I'd give it up if I could.

5

Nick, Jamie, and Maya are out in the waves with their boogie boards. From the waterline, where I'm standing alone, I can see them laughing. I can also see the occasional black seal head pop up like a dog's, pop down again. I scan constantly for shark fins, or try to, despite my sunglasses prescription being from the Cretaceous Period.

The fall Jamie was four and Willa was not yet one, I asked Nick to drive me out to this beach. It was September, and we'd booked a single night at a motel with money we didn't have. "Just drop me off, okay?" I'd said to him. "Can you just drop me at the beach, and take the kids to get ice cream or something? Come back for me in an hour." "Of course," he'd said. He kissed me nervously before I got out of the car. He was terrified of me then. I swam and swam—clambered up to shore reluctantly, and only when I couldn't feel my legs anymore. The sky was the impossible blue of a blue crayon.

"You good?" Willa has come down to stand beside me, and she slings a lightly tattooed arm around my shoulders.

"Totally!" I say, and she peers into my face, dabs a tear away with her thumb.

"Are you crying because your bush has grown down to your knees?" I look down and laugh and decide to keep to myself the fact that my bush is actually *shrinking* now, of all ironic horrors. "Oh my god—wait," she says. "Is that where the word *bushy* comes from?"

"I think it's the other way around," I say.

"Oh, right." She nods. "Are you mad at Dad about something?"

"Not especially," I say, and she says, "Good," and bends down to pluck up a pearly, sherbet-colored shell—the kind we've always called *toenail shells*.

"You really don't need to worry about me," I say, and she says, "Agree to disagree. Do you want to come up and eat your lunch under the umbrella with me?" I do.

Despite the many cheerful photographs suggesting otherwise, I did not love lunch on the beach when the kids were little. They were so committed, it seemed, to getting sand in the cooler, sand in the chip bag, sand in the cherry bag, the cookies, the pretzels. They dropped their sandwiches into the sand, spilled my iced tea into the sand, poured sand over their own sweaty heads for no reason and cried. They stuffed their sandy baby fingers into my nostrils. They groped me with their sandy palms. They tracked sand over the towels and through my psyche. All I wanted was two unsandy seconds to swallow down their peanut butter and jelly crusts and call it a meal.

Now, though? Now I love lunch on the beach so much that I laugh out loud.

"What is it, weirdo?" Willa says, and I shake my head, shrug. "Just happy."

"You are really living your best life, Mom," Willa says a couple minutes later.

I really might be! I've stuffed an enormous handful of potato chips into my sandwich and I'm sitting cross-legged on one of our old striped beach towels, tearing off huge bites and drinking deeply from a can of beer. Some tuna blobs onto my bare leg and I scoop it up with a chip. I used to wear a long cover-up. I used to wear a swim skirt beneath it so nobody could see my pale, pocked thighs in the embarrassing uncovered walk from towel to sea. I used to cringe over all the bobbing bits of myself. In recent years, though, I've come to understand that if I sat out here completely naked, nobody would even notice me. Except Nick, who would probably say a friendly, "Rawr!" before asking me to pass him the grapes.

"I really don't care about my cellulite anymore," I say.

"Smart," Willa says. "I mean, from an evolutionary standpoint, that cellulite is probably saving your life." She takes a bite of her sandwich and keeps talking, oil from the peppers gleaming on her lips. "Think about it. Old women? What are they even good for?"

"None taken," I say just before she says, "No offense," and she laughs, chews thoughtfully.

"You're not making babies, so nobody needs to think you're hot. But maybe you're useful—you can take care of other people's babies, help keep them alive long enough to reproduce—so you're still genetically important." A piece of mozzarella slides out of her sandwich into the sand, and she picks it up, pours seltzer over it, pops the rinsed cheese in her mouth.

"And the cellulite?" I ask.

Willa holds up a finger, finishes chewing, swallows, and drains her can. "You need the cellulite as an energy reserve in case the patriarchs decide you're ugly and pointless and stop feeding you." She shrugs.

"Sensible. How good is your sandwich?" I ask smugly. I notoriously troll for compliments.

"Oh my god, so good!" she says.

"Does it *slap*?" I ask, and she looks at me levelly, says, "I'm not sure it *slaps*."

"Say it slaps," I say, and she says, "It slaps."

"Free bird, by the way." She points to the top of my suit, where one of my boobs has escaped. I could not love this child more.

"I had another dirty *Top Chef* dream," I say, and she says, "Ooooh! Tell me."

"There was, like, a coffee table book, kind of? With a photograph of a vulva made out of flower petals? Only it wasn't petals—it was slices of baloney. And Padma Lakshmi peeled one off and ate it."

"Mom." Willa blinks at me. "Mom, you are seriously the most bisexual person who has ever lived."

"I know, right?" I say. "I'm here. I'm queer. Get used to it."

The swimmers stagger back up to us, dripping and starving. There is much crinkling of foil and eating of sandwiches, cookies, chips, fruit, and then Jamie is digging in the big blue IKEA bag for the Kadima set. He finds the paddles but not the ball. "Oh my god, Mom, what is even in here?"

"What *is* in there?" I ask, curious. "Although I don't feel like I'm really the person who has to answer to the contents of the beach bag."

He's pulled out all the sand toys—the beach around him littered now with brightly colored pails and shovels, snorkeling gear, a rusted metal garden trowel, a plastic pour-over coffee cone, two miniature Frisbees printed with a clam-shack logo— and he's still excavating. "Why are there actual *rocks* in here?" he says, and Willa says, "Those are probably mine," but doesn't look over from the *New Yorker* she's reading now. "There's actual trash!" He holds up a ball of tinfoil, an Italian ice cup. "Why are we dragging all this shit to the beach every summer? Oh my god, there's a cinnamon Smencil!"

"What's a Smencil?" Maya asks.

"It's a scented pencil," Willa says. "Although it always sounds like a Jewish name to me. Like *Oh, we can't that weekend! It's Smencil's bar mitzvah.*"

"There's *another* Smencil," Jamie says. "Also cinnamon."

Maya peers over. "It's like a dig site," she observes. "All the strata of your childhood artifacts." Maya was an archaeology major in college and works now at the Natural History Museum in New York. She's the Invertebrate Collections Manager and talks a lot about mussels and fossils and mussel fossils. Also, she's finishing up a paleontology PhD, *hashtag genius.*

"This is not an artifact from my childhood," Jamie says, and holds up a partially wrapped maxi pad.

"Give me that," I say. "Sorry. That's an artifact of my fertility."

As are you guys, I don't say to the kids. *As are these scars.* Nick catches my eye and smiles. I smile back.

"Eureka!" Jamie has found his ball, and he and his sister head down the beach to play, like the children they will always be.

6

Nick lets Willa and me out at the pond on the way back from the beach. He'll park at the house, drop off Jamie and Maya, and walk back to join us. It's not actually very far—we're just hot and sandy and lazy.

There are lots of kids in the little roped-off swimming area and a few clumps of slimy green growth. We are standing waist-deep.

"I definitely don't remember there being so much algae last year," Willa says, and a nearby goggled child says nasally, "It's actually *seaweed*."

"Thank you for inaccurately boysplaining that to me," she says, and he says, confused, "You're welcome."

"I feel like I'm going to have an actual biology doctorate one day and men of all ages are still going to be taking it upon themselves to miscorrect me," she says.

"That is almost certainly true," I say. "Let's swim out."

We duck under the nylon rope and paddle to the middle of the pond with our pool noodles. The kettle ponds are like black cereal bowls, ringed with trees. They're dark and deep and, once you get out far enough, perfectly cold. Maya once explained the way they were created eighteen thousand years ago, when the glaciers were receding—a number of years that gives me a little bit of vertigo.

"Watch this!" Willa says and gives me her pool noodle to hold while she does an underwater summersault. I cheer when she pops back up, and she laughs.

"Am I going to be a child forever?" she says, and I say, "I hope so!"

"Yikes!" she says suddenly, and I say, "Snake feeling?" and she nods. We are both terrified of snakes and frequently scare ourselves by imagining we see or feel one. I held her here as a baby, willing myself not to scream whenever something brushed my leg underwater. But my phobia leaked into her anyway. As a preschooler, Willa splashed and shrieked with her little water wings on: "A snake! A snake!" And the horrible truth is? Sometimes there really were snakes. Sometimes there are.

Willa wrote her college admissions essay about this pond, and I loved it. It was about all her layers of memories and experiences: she learned to swim here; she was happy here, and also anxious; Jamie taught her about molecules while they lazed in the shallows; my mother showed her where the blueberries grew at the water's edge; she came out to us here. In the version of the story she likes best, she splashes up to us to announce her gayness and I say, "No duh." This is not strictly true, but close enough. It was such a good essay.

"Do you think it represents enough about her leadership potential or whatever?" Nick had worried. "Isn't that what they always want?"

"Nah," I said. I'm a writer and have done some freelance work in college admissions. "I think the colleges are slowly realizing that admitting entire classes of leaders isn't actually going so great, from a practical standpoint." *Who the fuck is supposed to follow?* I didn't say. Because I was so placid!

"Okay, good. So the essay's not too . . . eccentric?" Nick said.

"It's about connection. Relationships." My commitment to placidity disintegrated, the bits of it coalescing to form a profane torrent. "Fuck them if they don't like it. Like, they can go and actually fuck themselves. Is there a better kid they're hoping to get than Willa? I don't fucking think so. Fuckers."

"Okey doke, then!" Nick had said, to make me laugh. And I did laugh. Also, I peeled off all my clothes because I was having *a massive fucking hot flash.*

"Oh, look! It's Dad!"

Nick is waving to us from shore and walking into the water to join us.

He greets us with a quiet hello, and the pond carries the sound directly into our ears.

"That's the refraction of sound waves," Willa says. "It's so cool. Oh, remember when we used to play Summer Olympics here?" I do.

"Jamie always invented the funnest relays and contests and stuff." This is true. Jamie would make us doggy paddle with a rock in each armpit or with our butts sticking all the way out of the water. We held medal ceremonies on the beach. We ducked our heads while Jamie placed strings of metallic plastic Mardi Gras beads around our necks and sang the made-up anthems of our imaginary countries. One time, when the kids were already in high school, we were in the middle of a particular event when the girl Jamie liked from home happened to stroll onto the beach. "Hey, Jamie! What are you guys doing?" she said, and Jamie tugged the crown of water lilies off of his head and said, "Just chilling."

"But remember how I always complained about the teams not being big enough?" Willa sighs.

"I do," I say.

"I wanted more sisters and brothers," she says. "I wanted more kids."

"I know you did," I say.

I did too.

7

I'm looking through the medicine cabinet for the poison ivy scrub. There's the same bottle of Jean Naté after-bath splash that's been here as long as we've been coming. The same crumpled metal tube of Bain de Soleil, SPF 0—oh, glorious orange gelée of my past!—which I will uncap later so as to breathe in the scent of my future squamous cell carcinomas. There's half a bottle of Robitussin, an unwrapped pink seashell-shaped soap, a box of assorted Band-Aids with only the tiny little strips left, and some actual talcum powder made from talc and, one has to assume, asbestos.

"I don't think there's any Tecnu here anymore," I say to Willa, "but I'd be happy to pop out and get some." Walking back from the pond, she'd leaned into a patch of brambles to pick a ripe blackberry. She noticed the poison ivy everywhere only after she was back on the trail.

"Maybe I don't need it." She's perched on the edge of the tub, looking at her phone. "It says here that rubbing hard with a washcloth and any kind of soap is more effective than a specialty removal product. Wow," she adds, deadpan. "I can't believe capitalism would sell us something we don't strictly need!" She runs the bathtub faucet and sets about scrubbing her shins and ankles. Chicken sits upright on the bath mat to supervise, reaching out a white mitten every now and then to bat at the dangling edge of the washcloth. The first summer we brought him here, he shimmied up the shower curtain and wedged his kitten self into a narrow gap between the bathroom ceiling and the roof. Nick had to hold Willa up so that she could reach her small hand in with a treat and lure him out. I ask Willa if she remembers, and of course she does, even though she was only five or six at the time. "Don't remind me how old he is, though!" she says. "You know I don't like to think about it."

"Same," I say, even though I think about it anyway. I sometimes worry that if a genie suddenly steamed out from the teakettle and granted me eternal life for five people of my choosing, Chicken would be one of them. This is one of the lesser secrets I keep.

In the kitchen, the blender is whirring. Jamie is cooking up some happy-hour fun: frozen coconut mojitos with tons of lime and massive sprigs of mint he's plucked from the planter outside. "Who wants?" he says, and everybody wants—though Willa just wants a virgin one. "You guys, can I take the car later?" she says. "I'm meeting Callie."

"Who's Callie?" I say.

"Surf-shop Callie," Jamie says, glugging rum into four of the five glasses and winking at his sister.

We sit on the deck, where Nick has put out the smoked bluefish pâté and a sleeve of Ritz crackers, a wedge of Brie for Willa.

"Okay, so you make an exception for clams but not for bluefish?" Jamie says to Willa, and she says, "Right."

"Why clams, though?" he says. "I mean, if you eat clams,

that's, like, twenty-five lives right there. But you could eat, like, fifty strips of bacon and it would only be one single pig."

Willa nods, holds up a finger while she finishes chewing. "I know. I've thought about that too. But can you picture *Charlotte's Web*, only Wilbur is a *clam*?" Jamie acknowledges that this would likely be a less heart-wrenching story.

I watch Maya a little to see if she's actually drinking her drink—and she is. She at least seems to be. My hair is wet from the pond. Willa is still wrapped in a towel after getting her poison ivy sorted out. The evening sky is turning from blue to the palest pink and it is all so, so good.

"Why is this so delicious?" I ask about the pâté.

Jamie looks at the ingredients. "Horseradish?" he says. "Lemon? Vacation?"

It's always so easy with grown kids! Okay, that's not true. They struggle and stray and are sometimes heartbroken. They can bristle, take offense, go silent. They chafe against the very fact of you, the parents—against the judgment seeping out of you even while you're busy impressing yourself with your own restraint. Still, there's so much joyful contentment, at least compared to how it used to be. Because it's such absolute chaos, vacationing when they're small. You need to carry not only the babies themselves, the toddlers, everybody as breaded with sand as a gritty scallopini, but also all the paraphernalia: the assorted pads and cloths and clothes and bottles of whatever they need bottles of at any given moment. Juice boxes and a shade tent and the pacifier and the lovey (the less-loved lovey, if you can get away with it, in case the unthinkable happens, and it will). Yes, the baby laughs hysterically when you say the word *boing*, but you might spend half your day balling up sodden swim diapers or coaxing somebody into the port-a-potty. You might end up actually *role-playing* how to use the port-a-potty, right there in the parking lot—"and then the door will close, but you won't have to worry about latching it because I'll be right outside"— realizing, only after it's too late and they're crying and crying about the terrible smell, that it would have been quicker to drive them back to the cottage to use the actual flush toilet. That it would have been quicker to get a degree in aerospace engineering and build a rocket so they could poop directly onto the odorless surface of the moon.

Despite the cheerful photographs and tearful nostalgia, despite how you look wistfully back and see only your own defined collarbones and prettily tanned shoulders, the children rosy and perfect, you probably spent the entire week discouraging a furiously determined someone from biting into a stick of butter.

Then there are the true kid years. The children can locomote effectively. They can relieve themselves without a lot of drama and maybe even carry their own boogie board or a single pail. They can play mini-golf, tell a decent knock-knock joke, build a sandcastle, read a *Magic Tree House* book in the shade, put cheese on a cracker. Their teeth are falling out all over the place, but they're good company and still innocent, still thrilled about seashells, hermit crabs, and the bubblegum eyeballs on the *SpongeBob Squarepants* popsicle they pick out from the ice-cream truck. Maybe a bubblegum eyeball falls off onto the beach and they cry a little, but they actually get over it now instead of needing you to bury the eyeball in the sand and build a seashell monument where people can come to weep and keen like the eyeball is Elvis interred at Graceland.

These older little children might complain all day about a quarter-mile bike ride you suggested, but they still go to bed early, clean and damp-haired in their striped pajamas. After reading to them about a shipwrecked mouse and a friendly whale, you can sneak out to the deck with their dad and a nine-dollar bottle of rosé.

Later still, the kids learn Settlers of Catan, and your vacation falls into place. Yeah, they rage at you about privacy and boundaries because you knock to ask if you might sneak in and pee while they monopolize the bathroom for a mysterious hour. They find much of your behavior *sketchy*, even when you're way out in the Atlantic Ocean. You might be distracted by an angry cyst on their forehead—the way it glows in the sun like a warning: *Code red! This is a menstruating teenager! Retreat!* There might be Laffy Taffy wrappers and Dorito bags on every surface when you wake up in the cottage, a whiff of something funky in the air that maybe isn't only hormones and sweat. Is it weed? Is it an actual skunk? Nobody knows.

But this? These grown kids, after your own life has grown so quiet? ("Dad and I defrosted the chest freezer" is an actual text I once sent in response to a question about our weekend and how it was going.) The kids who shake cocktails and fry squid and drive to the corn stand and tell funny stories about the kombucha tap at work? I had no idea it would be this good. If you'd have shown Nick and me videos of this while we were still squatting on the beach to comfort a crying someone about the sand having a *shrimp smell*? We would not have believed you.

"Is this new this year?" Jamie asks, and raps his knuckles on the glass tabletop. "Didn't it used to be plastic?"

"I think it was new last year," Nick says. "Or maybe they replaced all the patio furniture during the pandemic?"

"I think they actually got rid of those white chairs a couple years ago," Maya says.

"Is it weird that I'm kind of offended when they replace stuff?" Willa says. "Like, they didn't even consult with us!" Last year they swapped out the weird bamboo-frame, hibiscus-patterned love seat for a sleek and comfortable sofa bed, and everybody had mixed feelings. But the tippy bamboo coffee table is still here, at least—the one with such wide gaps between its lashed-together sticks that the TV remote falls through to the floor. You can't even balance a can of seltzer on it. "I love this table," Willa always says, affectionately. "It's so pointless."

"I have that too," Jamie says. "I feel like it's our shared place. That we share with them. And I don't love all the new LIFE'S A BEACH driftwood tchotchkes."

"Same," Willa says, and I laugh. People who insist that you should be grateful instead of complaining? They maybe don't understand how much gratitude one might feel about the opportunity to complain.

Jamie and I gather up the plates and glasses and head back in through the sliding glass door to make dinner.

"Are you sure this is going to be okay with you—the smell?" I yell out to Maya, about the sea scallops I'm blotting dry with a paper towel. "You're really okay?"

"Totally fine!" she yells, and I decide not to worry about her.

Jamie is making his famous potato salad—the one with heaps of fresh dill and chopped dill pickles and celery, the potatoes dressed while they're still warm so they absorb all the herby, salty vinegar. I put water on for green beans, search for the cast-iron skillet in the drawer beneath the narrow stove. Jamie and I keep colliding, opening drawers into each other's hips—the kitchen is so tiny. Nick sets the table. He reaches around us for dishes and silverware, lights the votive candles he's dug out from the board-game cabinet. The girls are on the bed, watching TikToks about somebody who filled his basement with water and turned it into an eel habitat. Or maybe I didn't hear that right. "Do you want this grilled tofu I brought from home?" I ask Willa, and she does.

Once the potatoes are out of the colander, I put the beans in the water, turn the heat under the skillet to high, salt the scallops. I pour a little olive oil in the pan, add a knob of butter, which bubbles and browns immediately. The scallops sizzle and spit in the pan like they're supposed to, send out a plume of briny steam. Jamie drains the beans for me, butters and salts them, grates on a little lemon zest, squeezes in a bit of the juice. By the time he's quartered another lemon for the seafood, the scallops are deeply browned in the sticky way we love.

"Cheers, my darlings," I say when we sit down. "Thank you for being here with us! This is such a special week." We clink glasses and Maya says, "It really is," and—does she?—winks at me.

MONDAY

8

I open my eyes to sunshine pooling around us in our loft bed, the skylight a brilliant square against the unfinished wood ceiling. Nick is already awake, propped up and reading a magazine. I wrap an arm around his waist.

"If it weren't for the *New Yorker*, I wouldn't really know much about rap music," he says. "Which seems wrong somehow." Indeed.

"It's only Monday!" I say. I say this every year. This is the part of our vacation where I feel like the week will never end. Like it's just going to stretch out luxuriously this way for the rest of time. It won't last, though. Later I'll cry, "How is it already Friday?" and everyone will nod and sigh because I ask this every year.

Nick tosses his magazine to the floor theatrically, removes his reading glasses, and tunnels under the covers, under my T-shirt. I feel his hot breath on my belly. He taps me with one finger over my underpants, says, "Testing, testing. Is this thing on?"

In a pie chart of Nick's personality, Dad Jokes would be, like, seven of the eight slices. He responds to every text in our family group chat with a GIF from a comedic film that is usually *Elf*: Buddy the Elf jumping up and down, yelling, "Santa's coming!" if you're excited; Buddy the Elf bent over a rabid raccoon—"Does somebody need a hug?"—if you're sad about something. He'll make the occasional exception, though. Like, if you texted him that your plane had been hijacked, he'd probably send you the scream face from *Home Alone*.

His entire, very large family is like this. In the place where other families might have conversations, catch each other up about their lives, he and his five siblings swap lines from *Fletch*. From *Caddyshack* and *Princess Bride*. I'm always Sherlock Holmesing around them all with my emotional magnifying glass, trying to figure out if anybody has any actual feelings and what those might be. Sometimes I'm more direct. "Do you think Nicky and I are going to hell?" I once asked his devout sister—this was before we were married. We were in the hired car on the way to their grandmother's funeral, come to think of it. "You betcha!" she said. (Marge from *Fargo*.) "Actually?" I said, and she sighed, grew serious and sad just long enough to say, "*Actually*."

At some point during the grinding hours of labor that preceded Jamie's birth, Nick quoted a line from *Three Men and a Baby*, and I thought, about my marriage to him: *I have made a grave error*. But then I woke in the night and saw him by the hospital window. Our swaddled baby was tucked into the crook of his elbow, and Nick was whispering to him about the moon and the stars.

"Honey," I say quietly, tugging on Nick's hair. "Nicky. Stop. When I turn my head to the side, I can literally see Willa sleeping."

"So don't turn your head to the side," Nick says, sliding his thumbs under my waistband.

"Stop, stop," I say, and he clambers up beside me, sighs. "I can't," I say. "I'm sorry. But also? The fact that you can? It's annoying to me. It's like our parenting lives are nonintersecting. You wanted to have sex that time Jamie was in our bed with *pneumonia*! He had a hundred and four fever."

"Did I?" he says. The bruise around his eye is green now. "That was twenty years ago, but yeah—it sounds plausible. Win some, lose some."

Here's the thing about menopause, though, that I don't entirely understand. We'll exchange a few words like this? A seemingly slight disagreement? Only then rage fizzes up inside my rib cage. It burns and unspools, as berserk and sulfuric as those black-snake fireworks from childhood: one tiny pellet, with seemingly infinite potential to create dark matter—dark matter that's kind of like a magic serpent and kind of like a giant ash turd.

"Why do I have to be in charge of every single thing?" I hiss.

"Honey," Nick says. He does not say, *Like highway driving?* which I have done literally not one single mile of in the course of our many years together. He does not say, *Like the gutters? Like being chill when things are going wrong?* He knows enough to placate me now. "Honey, okay. Sorry. I'm just flirting. It's okay."

"Don't placate me," I say quietly. "It's not *okay*. Jesus fucking Christ. I'm right to be mad!" Am I, though? I fucking *am*! "It's so annoying the way women have to do all the hard things and take care of everybody and pay attention to everything all the time. And then be soft and open and fuckable. It's infuriating!"

I'm so mad now I'm crying, and when Nick lays a hand on my thigh, I push it away. Even though I want him to comfort me. I want him to scoop me up and rock me. I'm furious. I'm exhausted. I don't really sleep anymore. Like, at all. "I'm not even totally sure what I'm mad about," I say, and he wraps his arms around me. "Do you think we should split up?" I whisper, crying, and he whispers back, angry himself finally, "Jesus, Rock."

"I'm sorry," I say, still crying. "Something is seriously wrong with me. Also, it is so fucking hot in here I'm going to die." Nick and I have been together since we were practically kids, and in that time he has gone handsomely gray at the temples while I have gone full whiskered harpy.

"You wish you knew how to quit me," he says (*Brokeback Mountain*). "But you can't." It's true. Even with all the nonintersecting forms of communication, I can't quite fathom a life apart. He is sometimes mysterious, this man, and often maddening, but he smells like home.

Nick, the most patient person I have ever known, kisses my wet face. He takes my hand. "Come with me," he says, and climbs out of bed, stands. "We can have make-up sex in the outdoor shower."

"Ew," Willa says. "I heard that. Also, Dad? I can see your naked ass and don't want to. You guys, I had a dream about the song John Jacob Jingleheimer Schmidt."

"You are definitely your father's daughter," I call down. If I sleep at all, I dream that I'm trying to punch urgent numbers into my phone except I have stump hands and also I am likely naked from the waist down because somebody darts by wearing my undies.

Nick is pulling on his running shorts, which makes me groan because I hate running but I'll probably go with him. "Is it a song about alienation?" Willa calls up. "Like, you meet yourself and you don't even realize it's you? I never really thought about it before."

"Same," I say. Nick walks gingerly down the metal staircase, which hurts our heels now. We both have plantar fasciitis, a punishment for years of mocking all the special foot remedies in the Hammacher Schlemmer catalogue. "Why do these people need so many special kinds of footwear?" we wondered aloud, like the young fools we were. "What's an *orthotic shower shoe*? Why a *biomechanical footbed*?" Now we have several pairs of therapeutic flip-flops and share an enormous, adjustable stabilizer boot that we occasionally wear to bed. I picture an extraterrestrial squinting down at us from space, pointing to our strappy plastic sleep boot. *What the hell is* that? Then again, I picture them peering at the Lycra-wrapped people staggering across a CrossFit gym with car tires roped around their waists. *What the hell are* those?

"Do I have to run with you?" I groan down to Nick, and he says, "Of course not!"

"Nicky, no! Say I have to."

"Oh, okay," he says. "You have to." I can hear Chicken complaining to him about his breakfast and why he doesn't have it yet.

"But do you wish I wouldn't?" I say.

"Mom, try not to hurt your own feelings for no reason," Willa says. This is sensible advice.

The bike path is hard under my feet, and I have the horrible juddering sensation we call *bag of bones*. "I feel like I got airlifted here directly from the catacombs," I say, and Nick laughs. I want to complain about my knee, but Nick is a physical therapist and if you're not careful you'll find yourself on the floor performing a series of terrible exercises. Also he will get out the innocuous-sounding *foam roller* that is actually a complex pain device designed by people who hate everybody. I've seen enough videos of cats terrorized by cucumbers to know what my face looks like when I suddenly see the foam roller.

Happily, there are many excuses to stop running and inspect our surroundings: beach plums (unripe), wild cherries (ripe), and rafts of mushrooms including the turmeric-colored, very delicious chicken of the woods. My English mum was raised by terrible nuns during the war. All those hungry, motherless girls searched the woods for wild edibles, which the convent cook prepared for them in secret. Foraging is my birthright. It might also be a weird kind of inherited trauma.

The self-righteous bicyclists pass us irritably, hunched over their handlebars, neon spandex gleaming. "It's the Cape Cod rail trail, folks!" Nick says quietly. "It's not the tour de *frawnse*." Nick's bursts of good-natured crankiness are a balm to my soul.

I complain to Nick about the most recent conversation I had with my dad. We'd been talking about the kids—specifically about a college science prize Willa had recently won. "Jamie used to be my favorite," my dad said enthusiastically, "and he's a good kid, but these days it's Willa."

"Jesus, Dad," I said. "Stop."

"I'm just saying!" he said. "They're both great kids, but I'd pick Willa."

"You don't have to *pick* anybody," I said. "It's not *Sophie's Choice* every second. Just enjoy them."

"No, Rachel," he said, prickly. "You always have to pick somebody." And that had been that.

"He's just wrong," Nick says now. "He's imperfect. This is not new information. It's okay. You still get to love him."

"I do," I say. I stop running to bend over, put my hands on my thighs. "I adore him."

"Your dad's the best," Nick says affably.

"But he's so annoying," I say.

Nick stops next to me and puts a hand on my sweaty back. "As are most people," he says, and this is too true to argue with.

"Nice," Willa says. We're back and I've unwrapped a bright shelf of mushrooms from my T-shirt. The big kids—as I continue to call them—are still asleep, but she wants to do something with us. "Anything," we tell her. "Gay watching in Province-town?" she muses. "Perfect," we say. "The Brewster library book sale?" "Either is great," we say. "Or the bay beach for hermit crabs?" Totally. Yes. All of it.

We've been coming here so long that the experience is deeply layered for her—the matryoshka doll of herself popping open, all the little nested selves tumbling out to see what's fun. The young adult with her sleekness and her DYKE tattoo; the school kid obsessed with animal-shaped erasers and *The Hunger Games*; the toddler with her potbelly and halo of fine, sandy hair. Everybody wants a say. I feel like this too. I was twenty-nine when we first came here. Twenty-nine! Closer to her age now than to my own.

"Bay beach," she concludes. "I was actually in P-town last night." Okay! Nick raises his eyebrows at me, smiles. "And we should save the book sale for a rainy day."

I've already slivered the mushrooms, and they sizzle when I add them to a panful of hot butter. I pluck out a few bugs that crawl out in the heat, toss them out the sliding door. The nickname of this fungal species is "sulfur shelf," and they have a faint eggy smell that I like. I sprinkle them with salt, grind lots of pepper into the pan. They give up all their yellow liquid, then bubble and dry out, brown a little in the fat. I tip them out onto a plate, squeeze a lemon over them, find three forks, and head out to the sunny deck, where Nick has opened the umbrella and has my coffee waiting for me in the shade.

"I love you so much!" I say, lifting the mug, and he shakes his head, whiplashed.

"Well, then, as long as you don't divorce me, we should be good."

9

The short version of make-up sex in the outdoor shower is that it doesn't happen. I get a splinter in my palm. I get a cramp in my calf. I can't stop laughing. And there are mechanical difficulties. Anatomical impossibilities. We're like bungling preschoolers with a shape sorter, and you're shaking your head: *That's never going to go in there.* My vag suddenly decides to impersonate aquarium tubing. A drinking straw. "You're definitely wet," Nick says, poking an exploratory finger into me. "Just kind of . . . narrow." "I feel like you just probed me with a meat thermometer," I say, and he laughs, shrugs. His half-mast cock droops lower. He smiles, as handsome as a movie star. He sings "Like a Virgin" to me. I sing him the chorus of the *Titanic* shanty: "It was sa-ad when the great ship went down!" We soap each other's back and bum amicably, towel off in the sunshine.

"It's the thought that counts," I say.

"Kind of," Nick says. I know he's thinking that the road to celibacy is paved with good intentions, but I just don't even care that much. I mean, I care *in theory*. But our experiences diverge. My body is a dangerous reproductive neighborhood.

I once squinted at an ultrasound with my mystified gynecologist until she clapped and said, "There!" and pointed to the IUD tipped over at the edge of my deflated party balloon of a uterus. "Probably not a great fit for you," she said, adding, superfluously, "birth-control-wise." Indeed it was not. None of it was. I have had allergic reactions, in the vagina, to latex, lambskin, spermicide, and the ointment I used to treat a vaginal allergic reaction. I have had so many urinary tract infections that I know the clean-catch urine sample instructions by heart, verbatim. *Separate the labia with the thumb and forefinger of one hand*—YES, I KNOW. JESUS. I have had so many yeast infections that I know the Monistat suppository instructions by heart, verbatim. *Pull out both parts of the applicator and throw away (do not flush)*—I WON'T FLUSH. MY GOD. I'm supposed to drink unsweetened cranberry juice, but it gives me heartburn. Instead I take a daily friendly-flora supplement, and every single morning I see the name on the bottle—FemBiotic—and hate everyone.

I weep and rage during sex. I cling to Nick's neck, sob, "This is how we made the babies!" I fill up, spill over with nostalgia. Loss. And Nick just comes and comes, all cheerful, if occasionally faltering, hydraulics. Sex is still about *pleasure* for him. It is not a holy act of grief-stricken joy. It is not exhibit A in a PTSD trial.

"Do you still think of yourself as queer?" Willa asked me recently. "I mean, is that the sexuality you most identify with?" The *sexuality*! Jesus. "Daddy and I have been monogamous for so long it's kind of hard to know" is all I could think to say. "Ew," she said. "Daddy."

. . .

When we get to the beach, Willa runs to the water with her pail. I'm so in love with her that if we were marsupials, I'd be stuffing her grown self back into my pouch. *You're fine!* I'd say to my leggy, complaining kangaroo or my cranky eucalyptus-scented koala. *Get in there and be quiet.* Instead I take her picture with my phone. She wades through the shallows, bending down to scoop up the hermit crabs that are scuttling away, darting along the bottom from seaweed clump to seaweed clump like spies in a spy movie. "Hello, little friend!" she says to every crab she meets. She holds them close to her face, talks to them gently.

In the Cape photos from when the children were little, I'm squinting grimly into the sun to make sure they're not drowning or choking on sand or catching spontaneously on fire. A deep, worried line divides my forehead in half. I remember not only the vigilance but also—more shamefully—the exasperation. "Just pick it up," Jamie likes to recall me saying to him, irritable, when he was a little skittish about a hermit crab he was hoping to hold. "It's got claws the size of dollhouse tweezers. You'll survive."

The year Jamie was eight, the kids dug a wide, shallow hole in the sand and filled it with water. They dumped in dozens of hermit crabs and watched, rapt, while they mingled and tussled. "Here, guys," Jamie said fondly, and tossed in an empty sea-snail shell. "In case anybody wants a new outfit!" "Oh, honey," I said. "That's so sweet, but I don't think it works like that." Only I was wrong. Because the wide, shallow pond turned into the fitting room of Filene's Basement. One crab shimmied out of her own shell, pinkly naked as a tiny boiled shrimp, and backed into the spare shell, reached around with her little claws to check the fit. After that, it was a free-for-all in the crab pool! It was musical chairs. The crabs patted themselves, craned their heads around, tried on one shell and then another, returned to their original shells, and popped out again, until, finally, all that was left was a single empty shell with a hole in it and a barnacle bulging from its top. "They left the worst shell!" Jamie observed, amazed. In the kids' memory of this moment—their own enthusiasm as pure and bright as a shooting star—I am probably checking them for ticks.

"Remember the year you told me to stop worrying about my flip-flops?" Willa, with her little pail full of crabs, has come to stand by me at the water's edge.

"Yes," I say sheepishly.

"'Just leave them at the bottom of the path,' you said. You said, 'Nobody's going to steal your flip-flops!'"

"I did say that."

"And what happened?"

"Somebody stole your flip-flops."

"Exactly," she says, satisfied. We call this style of childhood nostalgia the *catalogue of grievances*.

"Oooh, are we reminiscing about Mama's failures?" Nick says cheerfully. He has walked over to join us.

"Just that one," Willa says. "Unless I think of others. Don't bandwagon, though, Dad. This is just my own personal dumping. You guys, if it was a secret, would you want to see someone get eaten by a shark?"

"Oh my god!" I say. "That's terrible! Willa! No! Not *eaten*."

Willa laughs. "Bitten?"

"I mean, maybe *nibbled*."

"Same."

"You are bad people," Nick says.

We wade out together for what feels like a mile, the low tide never higher than our knees. Along the way, we see a big brown crab scuttling across the ocean floor, a transparent jellyfish, the ruffly kind of seaweed that looks like lettuce, and an old white couple with a cheerful, purple-faced baby.

"Does the baby's face look purple to you?" the woman says to us.

"Barely," I say.

"I think she's just a little cold," she says to me. "Shit," she says to the man. "Let's try to warm her up before we bring her back. They're going to kill us."

Everyone's in trouble at the beach.

Eventually Willa announces that it's seltzer o'clock and we turn back.

On shore, we pass our baby friend, whose face has pinked up again nicely. We briefly mistake someone else's umbrella and chairs for our own until Willa opens their cooler and it's full of bananas and Mountain Dew. "Sorry! Sorry!" I yell to the banana eaters, who are coming up out of the ocean toward us, confused but smiling. "Wrong cooler!" And we skulk back to our own spot, where Willa digs around in our drinks. "Do you want this?" She holds up a can of hoppy beer. "Or this?" She holds up a can of wine. I'm trying to drink less, but also I want both of these things.

"Wine and then beer, in the clear," I say, trying to remember the unsickening order of things. "Beer and then wine, feeling just fine."

"Mom," Willa says. "I don't think it's both."

I shrug, pick the wine, watch the people wading out and back in their brightly colored swimsuits and human-colored bodies.

The fall Jamie was five and Willa was not yet two, Nick dropped me off at the beach to swim alone. He kissed me nervously before I got out of the car. He was terrified of me then. Up to my neck in the water, I peeled off my swimsuit and felt the clots slide out of me like jellyfish, back into their natural habitat. *Blood attracts sharks*, I thought, but dully. *Come and get me*, I thought, but I didn't mean it. I only half meant it. I dunked my head to cry underwater, salt to salt.

"You good, Mom?" Willa says now, and I turn from memory to face her. "What is going on with you? I have a diagnosed anxiety disorder. I really don't need another thing to worry about."

Nick looks up from his magazine.

"Oh, honey," I say. "I'm sorry. Don't worry about me! I'm totally good. I'm so, so happy to be here with you."

This is how it is to love somebody. You tell them the truth. You lie a little.

And sometimes you don't say anything at all.

But it's okay because the ice cream guy is ringing his bell from the path and the kids are all running up the sand to the truck, Willa among them.

"Our baby girl," Nick says. He takes my hand.

"Our baby girl," I say back and squeeze his knuckles.

10

"You don't all have to look away be-cause I'm having a hot flash!" I say. I'm on the clam-shack patio, pouring sweat and peeling off layers. The four people I'm sitting with turn their faces back toward me. "It's not embarrassing." Except, of course, it is.

"Hey, Mom," Willa says gently. "I don't think you can take that off." This is true. There is only a bra under the black cotton tank top I'm half out of. I pull it down again.

But why? Why does a hot flash feel so humiliatingly gy-necological? As if your twat is personally shoveling coal into a terrible furnace. "It's the endocrine system," I explain, because they need to understand this. "It's not *vaginal*."

"Oh god, Mom! Can you please not?" Willa grimaces. "Sorry, Maya."

"Sorry," I say. I take a long drink from my Painkiller cock-tail. "Not sorry. Also, I'm pretty sure Maya already understands what I'm like—and has heard the word *vagina* before." Maya nods, smiles at me. Nick has been holding out his hand for my reading glasses, and I take them off, pass them to him so he can see the menu without holding it all the way out in a different county.

"Remember when we were, like, eleven and Mom told us we would have to go down on our girlfriends one day?" Jamie says, laughing.

"Oh my god, Jamie," Willa says. "Don't."

"Okay, you were, like, fourteen. And I was right, though. Right?"

"Ugh, Mom." Willa rolls her eyes. "Yes, female pleasure, but also bodily autonomy, etcetera. Nobody *has to* go down on anybody."

"Why don't I come back in a minute?" our waitress says from behind me.

"Thank you," I say, and Jamie says to Willa, "Just because you lost your virginity while *Ratatouille* was playing in the background—" But she interrupts him.

"Stop," Willa says. "Let me figure out what I'm ordering. Also, can we talk about when Grandma and Grandpa are coming and what's going to happen?"

We can! But first we have to order our food or else, as Jamie used to say, how is it ever going to come?

This place being called a "clam shack" is like if Peter Luger were called "Burger King." It is so incredibly good and so incredibly expensive. Usually I have a panic attack about the cost, and Nick has to remind me that we come here once a year and eat lentils all winter atoningly. I order the striped bass even though I know the fillet is going to be the size of a postage stamp—the size of my stomach's tiny, weakened voice crying out for more. But it will be crisp-skinned and perfectly delicious. "Salad or fries with that?" the waitress says, and I laugh. She laughs too, writes something down that is, I have to assume, the word *fries*. She's been working here as long as we've been coming and is the best.

Willa orders the peach and burrata salad, the Mexican street corn, and a side of onion rings but only after confirming that she can eat some of my fries. Nick and Jamie are each getting the fried fisherman's platter, which includes cod, scallops, clams, calamari, and shrimp. (I stop myself from asking if they want to split one between them.) Maya hesitates. "Can I just get a green salad with grilled chicken?" she says. "Dressing on the side." *Eating disorder?* is probably in a visible thought bubble over my head because Jamie shakes his head at me. But then Maya asks for more bread and I feel a little better.

My parents are coming up from New York the day after tomorrow. Wednesday. They're staying two nights. "It's going to be a full house again, guys, I'm sorry." Everyone says they don't mind at all, that it's worth it to have the time together. "I guess we'll do what we did last year? Put Maya and Jamie on the sofa. Willa, we can put the air mattress next to our bed for you—or on the deck if you prefer and the bugs aren't too bad."

"Unlikely," Willa says about the bugs.

"I'm sorry," I say again. "We talked about getting them a hotel room, but then we left it too late. Also, I think they'd really rather be with us anyway." I'm not sure this is true, but it sounds right.

"I might spend a night in P-town if I can borrow the car again," Willa says. Given the septic situation in the cottage, this is not an unwelcome plan.

"Feel free to invite Callie to join us for dinner," I say, and she says, "Oh god! It's not like that." *So what's it like?* is a question I don't ask.

"Should we eat at the fish-and-chips place they like?" Nick says, and I say, "That's what I was thinking."

"Do you want me to make spaghetti and clams one night?" Jamie says. "Or we could get them to cook lobsters for us at the fish market, eat them at home. They always love that."

"Honey," Nick says to me. "Do you think your mom can handle a whole lobster?"

This is a good question. We've noticed a tremor in her hands the last couple of times we've seen her, although she pooh-poohed our concern. "I mustn't steep my tea so long!" she said cheerfully. Britishly. "It's the caffeine." "Mustn't you?" Willa had teased. "Shan't you?"

Maybe they're keeping secrets from me, my parents. Maybe a lobster is going to be too much for my mother to handle. "I don't know," I say.

"That's too sad," Willa says. "That scares me a little. Grandma maybe can't even eat a lobster? Is that, like, Parkinson's?"

"She might just be kind of old," I say.

"That scares me too!" Willa says.

"The loons," Nick says in a quavery voice, because why worry about someone when you can make fun of them in a Katharine-Hepburn-in-*On-Golden-Pond* kind of way? "Sorry," he adds.

"What about the clams, though?" Jamie says. "Too garlicky for Grandpa? Too much"—he hesitates —"shells and stuff?"

"Yeah, maybe," I say. "I wonder if we should just do some plain fish. They've got striper at the market. We could get some of those good cocktail shrimp to start. I'll make tartar sauce. Cocktail sauce. A tomato salad. We can have stars with butter and parm."

Willa claps, says, "Yay!" We only ever have the tiny star-shaped pasta—*stelline*—on the Cape, and it's one of her favorite traditions dating back to her toddlerhood. That and the little boxes of sweet cereal we still get here and only here, and which the kids have always traded in complicated rounds of drafting. "Can I swap you Cocoa Puffs for Honey Smacks?" Willa asked yesterday, and Jamie said, "Sure." "Jamie!" she scolded. "You have to wheel and deal or it's no fun." "Oh, okay," he said amiably. "Throw in your Frosted Flakes!" "Are you crazy?" Willa said. "No deal."

Our food is arriving now because we are the kind of people who like to eat one meal while planning at least two other meals that are occurring in the future.

We eat, talk. The kids catch us up more on their work lives: Maya has acquired a clam fossil from the Miocene Epoch that she's busy trying to date accurately. "How old *might* it be?" we wonder, and she says, "Maybe twenty million years?" That's *crazy*! "Dudes," she says, and shakes her head. "There are clam fossils from the *Cambrian* Period! That's, like, over five hundred million years ago." I float away into a gaping existential infinity crisis, float back to hear about Jamie's new account with a restaurant start-up called Corporate Salad. "Your salad comes in a compostable bowl made out of recycled money!"

"Actually?"

"No." He sighs. "But wouldn't that be so epic?"

Meanwhile, in the bumblebee lab where she's a summer intern, Willa is infecting the bees with a stomach bug and then making them shit all over the flower garden out back. "We're trying to figure out which plants offer natural protection from disease transmission. Picture norovirus spreading on a cruise ship. We're basically studying the doorknobs."

I try not to say, "You guys are such bright fucking lights I could die of blindedness!" I annoy them with my doting, I know, because they tell me so.

"You guys are amazing!" Nick says, and they smile at him. "Thanks, Dad," Jamie says, because Nick gets to say whatever he wants.

Maya is, I'm sorry to note, picking at her salad when she makes eye contact with me and laughs. "What?" I say, and she says, "Remember when Jamie and I were first dating? When you liked my Instagram post?" I slap my own forehead. He had told me about her—they'd met at a party—and I'd been stalking a little and accidentally hearted something. "Oh my god!" I said to Willa, who was lying in bed next to me. "I just liked Jamie's sort-of new girlfriend's photo of a crab cake." "No, no, no," she said, and grabbed my hand. She was laughing. "Mama. Mom. Don't. No, no! Don't unlike it now. You're just going to draw more attention to it. Oh my god, wait, now did you re-like it? Mom!"

I cringe now. "Sorry, you guys. I'm the worst."

I don't mention how just last night, in the scrolling insomniac dark, I'd read a vague Facebook post from someone I went to grad school with about a person in our cohort—his ex-partner, maybe? His best friend?—who had killed herself. I couldn't remember her full name, but when I googled "experimental poet Gabriela suicide Iowa" I got zero results. Because I'd actually typed this set of words not into a Google search but as a comment on my grieving classmate's post. I deleted it and held Chicken under the covers while I finished having an imaginary stroke. "Why am I like this?" I asked Nick in the dark. But he was sleeping, like people do.

Maya pushes her mostly full plate away, notices me noticing her do it, and pulls it back toward herself. "Rocky," she says, and I say, "I know, I know. I'm sorry, honey. Just eat what you want."

"She's just like that, Maya," Willa says, waving her corncob toward me for emphasis. "I really don't think she can help it."

"Thank you, baby," I say, and mean it.

TUESDAY

11

The molecular disturbance of an un-
well kid always wakes me up. Many parents—mothers—will
tell you the same thing. My eyes snap open and Maya is kneeling quietly by my side of the bed, pale as milk.

"Honey," I say. "What is it?"

"Rocky," she whispers. "Rock, can I talk to you?"

"Of course, of course." I sit up, stand up, pull on my jeans,
pull Maya up to standing. "Come outside with me."

We walk quietly on the path to the little pond—the one
we've always called Secret Pond—and sit on the bench there.
It's warm, but the sun is not all the way up yet, or maybe it's
just overcast. The sky is low above our heads—an oddly opaque
kind of pale blue with a dark shelf of clouds scudding and
swelling in the distance. There are little grumbles of thunder.
I sit quietly, wait for her to say it.

"I'm pregnant," Maya says.

"Oh, honey," I say. "Okay. Tell me more. Or don't. Tell me
whatever you want." I dig my fingernails into my palms to
make myself stop saying things.

Maya rearranges her limbs so that she's cross-legged on the

bench, facing me. Her golden-green eyes are the exact same color as Chicken's! I keep this observation to myself.

"I don't know what to say," she says. She twists her braided silver thumb ring but doesn't look down. She's got on just the littlest scrap of a white nightgown—or maybe it's a sundress?—and the weird light bounces off her shoulders, her thighs, the tops of her bare feet. I can already see the veins threading across her breasts, her body mapping out its plans for the baby. I do not tell her she looks like a fertility goddess.

"You don't have to say anything," I say.

"I mean, I would tell you, if I knew what to tell you." She laughs, shrugs, drops her hands into her lap. "I honestly just don't even know how I feel. Besides kind of sick."

"Yeah," I say. "I've been there. I used to throw up entire sleeves of saltines. Immediately. Like, you could have put them back in the package." I was pregnant with Jamie at my own wedding, as my mother was pregnant with me at hers.

She chuckles, says, "Yeah. The thing is, I wasn't trying to be pregnant. Get pregnant."

"I understand," I say.

"We're careful?" she says. "I mean pretty careful. I don't know. Maybe we're not that careful. Sorry. More than you wanted to know."

"It's fine," I say. "Don't worry. You're good. You're perfect."

A weird gray slit opens between the black cloud shelf and the milky sky, and a bunch of sunbeams shoot down from it like in a child's drawing of the sun.

"Oooh, crepuscular rays!" she says, and I say, "Okay, Stephen Hawking."

She laughs. "I don't totally know what I want to do," she

says, steady, and I nod. A few large raindrops bounce down around us and then stop.

"What are the main contenders?"

"Um, I guess the obvious ones? Have it. Don't have it."

"Duh," I say. "Sorry. Those are definitely the two. Do you know how pregnant you are?"

"Not very," she says. "Maybe seven weeks. Eight. I just did the test before we left New York."

"Okay," I say. "You've got some time to decide." I don't make a depressing joke about the Supreme Court.

"We're so young?" They're both twenty-four. "I mean, my frontal lobe is probably still developing. But also, not, like, so young that it's a no-brainer. I got pregnant in high school," she says and waves her hand. "Having an abortion was a super-easy decision then. I got it done during a free period between chem and Spanish." She laughs. "Those were the days!" Those probably really were the days! I have to take her word for it. Our past experiences seem to diverge.

Lightning zigzags over our heads, a bone-jarring boom of thunder right behind it. The rain starts again—heavy drops that smell metallic—and we pull each other to standing.

"Is Jamie helpful at all?" *Please, please, please*, I think. *Please let him be a graceful and compassionate partner to this beautiful person.*

"Oh. Yeah. No," Maya says. She shakes her head. "I haven't told him yet."

Jamie is going to kill me.

12

Last month at my doctor's office—when I went in to talk about menopause and how it is fucking KILLING ME—I had to fill out a new form. "Number of pregnancies?" it asked. "Number of live births?"

"That thing should come with a trigger warning," I said to my doctor from the crinkly paper table where I was lying on my back in a crinkly paper gown. She wheeled her little stool around to look at my face, nodded sympathetically, asked what she could do for me. I sat up so I could feel more like a human woman than like a pile of old ham slices wrapped in deli paper.

"My vag is kind of getting . . ." What? What was it getting? ". . . smaller?" I said.

"And you're using lubrication?"

"Yeah," I said. "But I feel like lubrication's not really the issue."

She nodded. "Vaginal atrophy is pretty common after menopause."

"*Atrophy?*" I said. "Like, it just withers away? Grim."

"Do you experience pain with intercourse?"

"I do."

"Yeah, that's from the thinning of your vaginal tissues." I pictured wadded-up Kleenex on the floor next to the bed. "There's a suppository you could try." She flipped through my chart. "Your insurance might not cover it. It runs about three hundred dollars a month."

I called my friend Jo from the parking lot, and she was furious.

"That's bullshit!" she said. Her barrel-aged rage is always a relief to me.

"I know!" I said. "Which part specifically, though?"

"All of it!" she said. "The cost. The fact that our pussies just kind of dry up and blow away and people are profiting from that. The fact that Viagra is so much fucking cheaper."

"Should I try it, though?" I said, and she said, "What do you have sex—like, twice a month? Three times? Three hundred dollars? That's quarter-season Red Sox tickets. Not to put a dollar amount on it—I'm sure it's great and all—but for a hundred bucks a pop? Probably no."

I laughed. "That's fair," I said. "I'm going to think about it. But also? How am I a feminist, an advocate for reproductive rights, *Our Bodies, Ourselves*, hear me roar, blah blah, and I am only just now learning about vaginal atrophy?"

"I don't know," she said, and I could hear her sigh. "Because they hate us, I guess. But also? Can we just, like, *call it* at some point? We're sticking shit up our twats and the guys are taking boner pills—I mean, could we take it all as a sign to just, like, give it a rest? Could we just *not*? I just saw an ad for men who want to *last longer*. Who wants a guy to last *longer*? *Finish up* is my feeling. *My library book's not going to read itself!*"

"We could send our vaginas out to one of those retired

police-horse farms," I said, and she laughed. 'Those poor old girls worked hard!' people will say. 'They deserve this.'"

"Fuck," she said.

"What?"

"I've got to pick my dad up from Elder Zumba. Kill me."

We hung up and I looked at the prescription in my hand. More treatment? Really? More things pushed up into my body?

Number of pregnancies?
Number of live births?

Sex has nearly been the death of me.

13

Back at the cottage now, Maya darts into the bathroom, where I hear the faucet running on full, with just the faintest gagging sound beneath. Willa's still in bed, on her side, but her eyes are open. She pats the mattress behind her, and I lie down. She pulls my arm up around her, wiggles back into me. Chicken jumps heavily onto the bed and staggers over to fall into the crack between us, lies fatly on his back like a dead purring walrus.

"Everything good?" Willa says, and I say, "Totally."

"Good," she says. "I don't like to have to worry about everybody."

"I know, sweetie."

"On account of my clinical anxiety disorder."

I squeeze her. There's a flash, and thunder shakes the cottage.

"Wow!" Willa says. "This is my favorite."

"Mine too," I say.

"All of us here together, safe, with the storm out there. I love it so much."

"Same," I say.

Willa rolls over to look at Chicken and parts his fur to inspect his tummy. "Whose cat nipples are these?" she teases.

"Hmmm? Whose crusty old cat nipples? Are you going to nurse your kittens, Chickenhead?" His purring turns into a long grunting sigh and she kisses his face. "Mom," Willa says in Chicken's voice. "Willa thinks my neck smells like cheese."

"Well, does it?" I ask him and he says, sheepish, "Yeah."

Maya emerges from the bathroom and lies down on Willa's other side. Willa rolls back over to wrap an arm around her, sings a little bit of the made-up spoons song we used to sing when the kids were little. "Just three little spoons spooning spoons the way spoons do," she sings. Rain pelts the roof of the cottage noisily.

"This is a very cozy sight!" Nick says from the top of the spiral staircase. "Make room for Daddy!"

"Oh my god, Dad! Please."

"Sorry," he says. "Who wants coffee?" I do! Willa does! Maya does not.

The bedroom door opens, and Jamie smiles, says hi, and joins us, squeezing in at the side next to Maya. Willa pulls up the blue velour blanket and sings a little more of her song to account for the extra spoon.

"If there were a pill," Jamie says, "and you could take it to feel happier—but you would be happier because of a pill— would you take it?"

"Um, Jamie? Mama and I already take that pill," Willa says, and Jamie says, "Oh, shit! Right. Sorry. I forgot." This makes me laugh. Jamie is so aggressively mentally well, but also appealingly apologetic about it.

"Why does Mama get to be *Mama* still?" Nick asks from the kitchen.

"Because mama's not gross?" Willa says.

"I'm not gross!" Nick says. "I mean. I'm not *super* gross, at least."

"No, no. Not Mama herself. *Mama* the word. And anyways, I'm trying to switch to calling her Mom so that I don't feel like my baby-est self around her all the time."

"Oh, honey," I say. "You can be your baby-est self around me!"

"I know," she says. "But I don't want to."

"Did we bring these toasted almond bars?" Nick is peering into the freezer.

"I don't think so," I say. "How come?"

"I'm thinking of eating one."

"That gives me a weird feeling," I say.

"That always gives you a weird feeling," Jamie says. "Because you feel like maybe the people who stayed here last week are trying to poison us. Like, they're playing the long game of booking this place back in October of last year so that they could plant a poisoned ice-cream novelty and kill us. Or poisoned plum jam. Poisoned ranch dressing."

"Okay, okay."

"Anyone else want one?" Nick says through a mouthful of ice cream, and the three kids reach out their hands.

Nick and I return to the loft bed to do our online word puzzles under the rainy skylight. The kids lie on the sofa bed, showing each other TikToks and laughing.

"Everything good with Maya?" Nick says to me quietly, and I shush him, wave my hand, say, "Yes, yes, fine." He doesn't pursue it. Nick's curiosity about feelings and the people who have them is fleeting at best.

. . .

The summer Jamie was four and Willa was not yet one, we were here—in this very bed, the baby asleep between us—when I told Nick I was pregnant.

"Wait," he said. "How?"

"Um, I think the usual way," I said.

"But you're still breastfeeding. Isn't that supposed to keep you from getting pregnant?"

"Ideally," I said. "But it seems not to have."

"It's so weird, because—"

I pressed my hand to the side of his neck. "Nick. Stop. I don't want this conversation to keep being about how surprised you are that we had sex and conceived a baby."

"Sorry." He regrouped. "That's exciting!" he tried, and I shook my head.

"I'm so tired," I said. "I haven't really slept since before I was pregnant with Jamie."

Nick nodded, looked away. He was nervous, which was both understandable and annoying. "Yeah," he said. "But by the time this one is born, maybe you'll be caught up a little."

"Because pregnancy is such a restful time," I said. "Also a toddler."

"We'll make it work," he said. I mean, what else could he really say? But the *we* enraged me.

"The same *we* who slept through the babies waking up every five minutes?"

"I'll try to wake up more," Nick said, chastened. "I'm sorry. Just wake me up. I'm happy to get up."

I sighed. "I know you are," I said. I was crying a little bit. It was so hard to try to describe this feeling. Of being captive. Captured. Crazy. Of being madly in love with a miniature person whose entire survival depended on my mammary glands. Or felt like it did—because, of course, there were other ways to feed a baby. But I was deranged with responsibility, vigilance. Love. Tiredness. Forty percent of my waking thoughts were about the children dying—the other sixty about sleep. I was ashamed of this demented pie chart. I still cried when I made up the guest bed for anybody: I smoothed the clean, dry sheet with my hand, pictured our friend or relative deeply dreaming, and cried. When someone went to bed in the book I was reading—climbed under the duvet and closed their eyes—I cried. I daydreamed about hotel beds. I daydreamed about being hospitalized. I daydreamed about running away. In a novel, I would have waved to Nick and the kids, headed down the beach to look for sea glass, and never, ever returned. Because I would be somewhere else, asleep.

"We'll make it work," Nick said again, and patted me.

"Don't *pat* me," I said, and he sighed in the way of a person with no good options for saying or doing anything right.

Now everybody sleeps for a bit—or maybe only Chicken and I do—and it's lunchtime when we get up again. It's still pouring out, and the windows are gray, but the honey-colored pine walls glow in a cozy way.

Eggs are scrambled with Pepper Jack; a pound of bacon is cooked crisp on the griddle; heaps and heaps of the good sourdough sandwich bread are toasted and buttered. We make individual mugs of strong, milky coffee, pour glasses of juice, crowd around the little kitchen table under the stairs. We pass the hot sauce, the salt, the previous renters' plum jam. We make more toast. We talk about the rain.

What do people want to do with what's left of the day? Jamie wants to play Settlers of Catan—*Seafarers* of Catan, more precisely—and Willa and Maya want to go to the library book sale. We agree that there is plenty of time for both things. While Nick and Jamie wash and dry dishes, I look in the fridge and scratch out a quick shopping list: milk, half-and-half, eggs. Butter and sliced deli cheese. Fancy cheese. Bread. Chips. Lemons and limes. Eating fruit. Beer. We'll do the lobsters tonight, pick up corn. There's a baseball game on TV that Nick and Jamie might watch part of after dinner.

We pile into the car to drive to the Ladies' Library, where the famous book sale happens for a couple of weeks every summer. It's massive and dank and unchanging, books shelved across the entire basement into regular categories like Fiction, Poetry, and Biography, and also irregular categories like Cape Cod Shorebirds, Historical Yarn Crafts, Lighthouses, and Barnstable County Cookery. Everyone fans out to look at different things: Willa sits on the floor in the Children's section to leaf through picture books; Nick reads a Woody Allen memoir in the Humor section (ew); Jamie and Maya look at books on design and architecture. Almost everything here is fifty cents, except for some especially large and dreary books about the Civil War that are ten dollars.

We've been coming here since the days of used board books with chewed-up corners: *Baby Faces* and *Water Babies* and *Babies for Days*—the kind of books where, every time you turn a thick page, your own baby cheers and claps. The kids have looked at *Minecraft* books here. *Magic Tree House*, *Railway Children*, *Harry Potter*. Books on Judaism and Buddhism and enneagram personality types. They've gotten atlases and art books and cat books and folders full of old-timey sheet music. Books of puns and knock-knock jokes. *Stone Butch Blues.* And they've brought home nearly countless believe-it-or-not-type books of strange facts and spooky stories.

I like to look at all the spiral-bound cookbooks from various PTA and ladies' auxiliary fundraisers of the past—the ones that call for Jell-O and canned salmon and canned ham and pimiento-stuffed olives and use them in delightfully thrifty and unappetizing ways. One chapter, called "Our Jewish Friends," contains a recipe for brisket browned in bacon fat (so probably not *close* friends). I always buy a few to read aloud from at the beach.

I skip the Pregnancy and Babies section because I don't trust myself not to burst into tears or say something weird to Maya. In Self-Help, I flip to the index in a suspiciously slim book about menopause. There is no "vaginal atrophy." No "atrophy, vaginal." The fact that there's a chapter called "Moods and You!" makes me want to actually bludgeon someone to death with a bottle of Zoloft. I slam it shut, return it to the shelf. The book I'm looking for would be called something like *Gynecological Trauma and Bitterness: Your Vagina Is a Fucking Husk*, but they don't seem to have it. They do, however, have the memoir I read last year by the robustly menopausal writer who trashes her career and fucks up her marriage and alienates all her friends and ends up living alone in her car. Absolute legend! I pick up a couple of novels so I won't end up rereading all the random books in the cottage about whaling and salt.

Willa's getting an American Girl book about friendship and a pamphlet about the Myers-Briggs personality test. Jamie is getting a partially used book of Mad Libs. Nick is getting a how-to book about building a deck. And Maya is getting two books of Mary Oliver poetry. "I can Venmo you," she says—laughs when Nick says, "Yes. Thank you, Maya. Please Venmo me one dollar."

Willa Myers-Briggses us all in the car on the way back, and we learn, essentially, that the women in our family have feelings and the men have reason and math in the place where their feelings would be. I must say this out loud because Jamie says, "I really don't feel like that's *what we learned*." Oops!

"Ugh, sorry. But you and Daddy—Dad—act like human relationships are basically calculus problems. Sorry, sorry. Ugh," I say. "Sorry! I'm just so"—what?—"mad all the time."

"I think we know that," Nick says, and I laugh.

"I'm not mad at you guys," I say. "I mean, you, maybe." I point to Nick. "I don't know."

"Remember what you used to say to Jamie and me when we were fighting?" Willa says. I don't. "Just because it's hard for you doesn't mean you're doing any work to make it better."

"Yuck!" I say. "That's so annoying."

Nick drives with one hand so he can take my hand with the other. From the back seat, Willa pokes her bare foot into our laced fingers. "I think I might need a little alone time," I say, and everybody laughs.

"Too bad, Mom," Jamie says pleasantly. "I don't think that's how this week is going to work."

WEDNESDAY

14

In my dream, the baby falls out of my arms in the ocean. I see his face receding into the clear depths, but when I grab at him, there is only water. I open my mouth to scream, and it fills with the sea. I open my eyes, breathless.

"For someone who sleeps so little, I really manage to squeeze in the nightmares," I say to Nick, who is awake and reading his deck-building book in the morning light.

"Mm," he says.

"Shit," I say. I have a headache and also a bad feeling. "Are we fighting?"

He looks down at me over the top of his reading glasses. His black eye is yellow now. "We are," he says.

"Fuuuuuck. What are we fighting about?" I say, and Willa yells up, "Toxic masculinity. Also, you drank too much and got super salty. Sorry, I'm eavesdropping."

"Wait. What?"

"While we were playing Catan," she says.

I have a fuzzy memory. Did I actually fight with Nick about the trading of wool for lumber? I am such an asshole.

"I really don't think I'm smarter than you," Nick says quietly. "I hate it when you say that."

"I'm sorry," I say, instead of *Oh my god, I said that?* "I don't really think you think that either. It's shorthand for something I'm angry about, but it's hard to describe."

"The patriarchy," Willa calls up, and I say, "Honey, can you not—just for a minute?"

"Okay, I'm putting my headphones on," she says. "But just FYI, you should probably apologize to Jamie too. You cursed at him when he built a shipping route that cut you off."

"Jesus," I say.

"I don't want to fight all the time," Nick says, and I say, "Me either," but I'm not entirely sure it's true. I want something. I want something to change. But what?

We were in couples therapy once, and Nick said, "I'm just happy the way things are," and I said, "Even though I'm not? That seems insane to me." The therapist agreed that it was a *problematic disconnect.* Sometimes I feel like in the Venn diagram of our relationship, our circles of experience don't even overlap. Which is a pretty weird Venn diagram of a relationship. Then again, I'm hungover and furious about something I don't even fully remember, so now might not be the right time to draw conclusions about our fundamental incompatibility.

"The lobsters were good at least," I say, and he says, "Ooooh. They really were!" The table had gone uncharacteristically silent while four out of the five of us bent our heads to the extraction of sweet and chewy lumps of meat, dragged them through deep puddles of melted butter, exclaimed over their briny excellence.

"It was a crustaceous *orgy,*" Willa says. "Sorry, sorry. I'm putting my headphones on for real now."

I take the book out of Nick's hands, lay it on his bedside table, drape myself on top of him, press my face into his spicy-smelling skin. "Forgive me," I say into his neck. "Forgive me quick, because my parents will be here soon, and I really don't want you to be mad at me while they're reminding you of all the ways I'm going to be even more annoying in thirty years."

"I forgive you," he says, and wraps his arms around me. *Do not blow it*, I beg myself. *Do not force this lovely person to leave you, even if he sometimes behaves like an alien accountant from a planet where feelings emerge like calculator tape and get read aloud with no inflection.* I love him, I do. Even though his emotional life reminds me of those touristy flat-penny machines the kids loved when they were small: put in your fifty cents and a penny, crank the gears—so much effort!—while the machine groans and shudders, and then: yay, a flattened penny. *Stop*, I tell myself. *Shhhhh.* I breathe in Nick's beautiful hair, silvering so sexily, snuffle along his firm and scruffy jaw, and am neurochemically rewarded with oxytocin, the bonding drug. I am bonded.

"You're like a truffle pig," he says affectionately.

"A truffle pig who is kind of a dick," I say.

"A truffle pig who drank too many mojitos and is a poor sport," he says.

In the bathroom, I open the medicine cabinet, looking for Advil. I unscrew a glass jar of Pond's cold cream to inhale the smell of every mother's 1975 face. There's an orange prescription bottle, which excites me for a second, but it's just the same boring acid reflux medication I take too. I find Tylenol, swallow three or four capsules with water hand-cupped from tap to mouth.

. . .

The summer Jamie was five and Willa was not yet two, I found some Vicodin in here and took it. The cramping was a good excuse, but it was mostly about oblivion.

"I'm taking these," I said to Nick, showing him the bottle: a name not mine, an expiration date from the past.

"Okay," he said. "But not, like, *all* of those, right?"

"Right," I said. "Can you be in charge of the kids?"

"Yes." Willa stretched toward me, reaching out from Nick's arms, and I kissed her rosy face and turned away. I craved the kind of sleep that you wake from feeling like you've been on the ocean floor, bloop-bloop-blooping slowly up to the surface only after many drowned hours. I laid a towel over the bed, lay on top of it beneath the too-bright skylight and the shuddering ceiling fan. I rolled onto my side and held the pillow over my head so I wouldn't hear the baby crying.

Willa comes in while I'm brushing my teeth, squeezes a giant blob of toothpaste onto her own toothbrush, most of which bloops onto the top of my bare foot. "Oops," she says, and rubs it off with the sole of her own socked foot. "Fshinkl weeya shoo shooboo," she says through a mouthful of foam. She holds up a finger, spits into the sink, says, "Sorry. I think I need a new toothbrush. Remind me if we go to the weird drugstore in town."

"I doubt you need a new toothbrush," I say.

"When this part turns from blue to white you're supposed to replace it," she says, pointing to the bristles.

"And you call yourself a critic of capitalism!" I'm wiping toothpaste off the floor with a square of septic-friendly one-ply toilet paper.

"Good point," she says.

"You basically *never* need to replace your toothbrush," I say, and she says, "That would be interesting advice if it weren't coming from a person whose teeth are basically in ruins."

"That's fair," I say. I definitely have more crowns and fillings than I do natural-born enamel.

I'm looking in the mirror at my hair. My hair! What on earth? It used to hang down in heavy, glossy waves, and now it sticks out of my head like a marshful of brittle autumn grasses. It is simultaneously coarse and weightless in a way that seems like an actual paradox, as if my scalp is extruding a combination of twine, nothing, and fine-grit sandpaper.

"I'm basically a human being made out of burlap," I say, leaning close to look at my pores, but Willa ignores me. She's peering into the disintegrating wicker hamper that's full of random bathroom supplies. "Dude," she says. "These maxi pads are total *mattresses!*" She holds up a plastic-wrapped wad the size of a romance novel. "Someone needs to get a DivaCup and get on with her life," she says.

"I think those are actually mine," I say, and she says, "No!"

"They are!" I say. "I think I left those here, like, twenty years ago."

"Wow!" she says. "Did you need a belt and special clips or whatever?"

"Yes," I say. "We had to weave them ourselves from flax and myrrh."

"So no," she says.

"Right," I say. "Just the regular adhesive strips."

At the very start of Covid, a friend of Willa's had asked me if I'd been alive during the last pandemic. "Which pandemic?"

I said, and he said, "You know, the flu." "The flu of *1918*?" I said, and he nodded. "No," I said, "I wasn't." "Cool cool," he said, still nodding. "Cool beans."

Those pads actually give me PTSD, I don't say to Willa now.

Jamie's door pops open when I push out of the bathroom, and I see his face and smile reflexively at it, say, "Hi, honey!" Only when he shakes his head do I realize that what I'm seeing is his face *on a computer screen*. His laptop is balanced on the dresser and his back is toward me, and I can see myself waving to him from the doorway in my underpants.

"Mom," Willa says from the bathroom. "Mom, Jamie's on a work call. Don't go in there." I pull the bedroom door closed and say, "Yes, I see that."

"At least you have a T-shirt on," she says, laughing. "Oh my god, Mom."

If these guys ever etch me up a tombstone, I hope that's all it says. *Oh my god, Mom.*

15

We're at the tram beach, where we've secured a spot not too far from the walkway, since my parents are planning to join us here after they arrive in town. While I'm looking at the waves, an ancient woman emerges from the ocean in a green wet suit with green flippers, her gray hair streaming behind her. She's like a mermaid. Like something from a Wes Anderson movie or a Greek myth. It's so, so good. Her specifically. Crone life in general. Also, it sucks.

Menopause feels like a slow leak: thoughts leaking out of your head; flesh leaking out of your skin; fluid leaking out of your joints. You need a lube job, is how you feel. Bodywork. Whatever you need, it sounds like a mechanic might be required, since something is seriously amiss with your head gasket.

You finally understand the word *crepey* as it applies to skin—although you could actually apply this word to your ass as well, less in the *crepe-paper* sense than the *flat-pancake* one. Activities that might injure you include ping-pong, napping, and opening a tub of Greek yogurt. Your hairline is receding in such a way that, in certain cropped photographs, you look like somebody's cute, balding uncle. You eat pepperoni pizza and, a half hour later, put a hand to your chest, grimacing like a person in an Alka-Seltzer commercial. You set a timer so you'll remember to take your proton pump inhibitor, and when it goes off your husband says, "It's reflux-o'clock somewhere!" You have under-eye bags. Jowls. *I Feel Bad About My Neck* makes total sense as a book title. You reflect on old TV commercials with new understanding: a crocodile slithering around in need of Lubriderm! Same! All the horrors that crept past without you ever looking up from your youth to take note of what they even were: They've circled back for you.

But then there are still other manifestations that you have never gotten a single rotten whiff of until they're happening specifically to you. Like the fact that your vagina sweats in the night. It perspires! This same vagina that so stubbornly refuses to produce any other type of moisture that when your gynecologist's nurse asks if you're sexually active, you laugh, shrug, make a so-so sign with your hand. "I'm going to put *yes* for that," she says, cheerfully. "Some active volcanoes haven't erupted in fifty years!" Your gums recede. You are covered in weird growths, as if a toddler has gotten a sheet of mole stickers and stuck them all over your breasts and armpits. Everything needs to be biopsied, except for the one under-boob skin tag that has actual tentacles, like an octopus; this is apparently so normal that the mammogram person barely looks when you show it to her—"That's totally fine!"—but then she puts a festive little donut sticker over it so the radiologist won't mistake it for a tumor. You have so many nipple hairs and most of them are white now. And your period does a kind of horror-movie swan song as if it is finally realizing its Freddie Krueger aspirations. For example, after a traffic jam over the Canadian border, you arrive in Montreal so drenched in gore that while you're talking to your Airbnb host a clot actually drops out the bottom of your pants into the snow. He looks at the spreading pink stain, says, "*Alors*," and hands you the keys.

You're so damaged by age, but so beautiful too, all wrinkled and rusty and tinted that . . . vintage brown tone. Even if you can't remember the word for it. Even if you're like, "Nick, what's that thing? It's brown?" And Nick looks at you over the *New Yorker* he's reading on the beach to say, "Um. Gingerbread?" And you're like, "No, no," shaking the tree of your memory but all that's falling out of it are the words *seep* and *steep*. "Gravy?" he says, because you have given him no more information. "Dirt?" "Seep," you say. "Steep. No, no. The brown color that's like, *Oh, that photo is so old!* Not stevia." "Sepia," Nick says, and you fall backward onto the sand because thank god. "Your swimsuit's inside out," Nick calls down, and you say, "Thanks."

Picture your pretzels spiraling out of the vending machine and stuck halfway. Every single item in your memory bank is that ungettable Snyder's bag, every movie star and city name and book title and adjective, and you're shaking the machine, trying to snake your hand up through the slot, pressing the coin return button in a rage. Forget it. Oh, you already have! Ha ha ha.

"What are you laughing about?" Nick says, and I put a hand up to shade my eyes. "Menopause, I guess," I say, and he says, "Yikes."

I'm mad about how mortifyingly public my reproductive life has been—while also being totally isolating. "At least I was spared the slapstick absurdity of getting an erection in, like, algebra class," I say to Nick, and he says, "At least that," looks down at me uncertainly.

A conversation like this might be a wolf in clown's clothing, and he knows it. My rage is like a pen leaking in his pocket, and before long there will be ink on his hands, his lips. But if we fight, I'm going to have to say more about the babies, the lying. About my sadness or Nick's. The older I get, it seems, the less I want to talk to anybody about their feelings or my own. Not in the usual way, at least. The responsible way. I want to behave badly and be immediately forgiven. Or maybe it's not that I want that—it's just what I do.

16

Hello! Hello! My parents are here! They've driven out to the house, and Jamie and Maya have brought them to us at the beach. They are so adorable, these white-haired people—my beautiful mother in her frayed chinos and a long-sleeved white linen shirt, my dad in his sneakers and socks and belted shorts and blue polo shirt—that I cry a little bit when I see them.

"Oh my! What a fuss!" my mother says from under her straw hat, but her eyes are damp too.

"Jesus Christ, this sand is hot as hell," my father says, hugging me briefly before plunking into a beach chair. "I can feel it through my shoes."

"I'm so glad you made it, Dad," I say to him, and then thank the kids for ferrying them.

"Our pleasure," Jamie says.

Willa hugs them both, and Nick hugs my mom, shakes my dad's hand.

"What do you need, Grandma?" Willa asks. "A chair? Something cold to drink? A sandwich? My mom made sandwiches."

"I'm just going to stand and stretch my legs for a bit, but

a cold drink would be lovely," my mother says. Willa hands her a can of seltzer, and my mother looks at the top of it and frowns.

"Be a darling and open this for me," she says, handing the can back to Willa. "They're so fiddly."

Nick and I exchange a concerned glance, which my mother catches us at. "Oh, stop, you two," she says. "I'm just old. This is not news to anybody."

Jamie and Maya swim in the ocean and the rest of us eat lunch. I've made sandwich-bread sandwiches from the good deli turkey and sliced Swiss, with coleslaw and yellow mustard on my dad's and just a little scraping of butter on my mom's and one single paper-thin slice of turkey, the way she likes it. After her war-rationed upbringing, she still seems to feel more comfortable if there's only the merest suggestion of filling. "Ah," she says, about her very skinny sandwich. "This is lovely!" We have the salt-and-vinegar potato chips they like, a quart of supermarket macaroni salad that we pass around with a single fork.

We sit in a semicircle of mismatched chairs and talk the way you talk on the beach: a mix of current events, the real or imagined spotting of wildlife, and gossipy observations about the people around us. Even though we've screwed the umbrella so far into the sand it's probably poking out of the ground somewhere near Australia, I panic when the breeze picks up. Nick's reluctance to apologize extends beyond our relationship, I have learned, when I've watched him retrieve our blown-away umbrella from someone's eye socket, saying only, "This is ours." I pile sand around the base while I listen to my parents talk to the kids.

"Willa," my dad says at some point, handing her his phone, "can you help me figure out why there's so much spam in my spam folder?"

"Mort, no," my mother says. "Put your phone away! You're going to drop it in the sand and ruin it."

"It's fine," he says. "Willa. Why?"

"Wait," she says. She chews and swallows. "What's the question? Why is there spam in your spam folder?"

"Yes," he says.

"Um, because it's your spam folder? I don't know, Grandpa. Is it bothering you?"

"It is," he says. "I don't like to look in my spam folder and see all these junky emails."

"Does it help if you don't look in your spam folder?"

"No," he says. "Then I just know they're all in there, and it's annoying."

"Do you want me to show you how to delete them?" Willa says.

"I would love that," my dad says, beaming at me because my daughter is an actual genius. "I do love spam, though," he adds, and Willa says, "Wait. What?"

"Actual Spam. The canned kind. Fried up with a couple of eggs."

Truth be told, this is not the first time he's enjoyed this particular bit.

"Oh, Mort, don't be revolting," my mother says, and he says, "Alice, have you even ever tried Spam?" My mother admits that she has not while Willa waits patiently with my dad's phone in her hand. "Grandpa, do you want me to show you how to delete these?"

"Oh, would you please just do it for me? I don't care enough to learn how."

The beach is a crazy quilt of colorful umbrellas and colorful beach towels and colorful swimsuits. I love it so much, even though the sun is very hot and the greenflies bite our ankles. People of all sizes stagger out of the frigid ocean, laughing. So many of them have tattoos, their chests and shoulders and arms inked all over like chaotic canvases. There are lots of white people with mottled red backs. There are young people scattered all around us in their luscious bodies, probably missing the point about collagen—which is that, fat or thin, their skin fits them exquisitely. Many people sit with books in their laps, only some of them actually reading. I myself sit with an unread *New Yorker* for so long that it makes a sucking sound when I move it, leaves an imprint of the back cover on my sweaty thighs. I doze a little under my baseball cap, listening to Willa and my dad arguing about the Black Lives Matter protests. At some point I hear my dad say, "Well, all I'm saying is if it were Jews smashing everybody's windows . . ." and I tune them out again. A couple of minutes later I hear my dad explaining the difference between a schlemiel and a schlimazel: a schlemiel is the kind of klutz who trips and falls into a shrub and scares a bird; a shlimazel is the person the scared bird shits on.

"I'll tell you what you really don't want to be, and that's a *schmegegge*," he says, and Willa laughs, says, "I don't even know what that is, but I really don't."

Jamie, meanwhile, is explaining to Maya how he thought the expression was "meet cute."

"Isn't it?" Maya says, and Willa says, "*M-E-A-T*. He thought it was 'meat cute.'"

"I pictured, like . . ." Jamie pauses. "A tiny little chuck roast. Smiling."

They laugh more, chat and argue, enthusiastically point out a topless old woman. "Oh, wait," I hear Willa say. "I think it's just an old man with titties. Okay, okay. Bless him. It's all good."

I'm listening to them while also eavesdropping on the slurring and heavily baseball-capped guys behind us, who seem to have drunk approximately ten thousand beers or been roofied.

"And do you want to know what was in the fucking koi pond?"

"Koi?"

"Yeah! It was fucking koi."

Their aerosol sunscreen blows over and gives me lung cancer.

"Oh, heyyyy," I hear Willa say, and I turn and cup my hands over my eyes to look. It's the cute surf-shop girl! She's wearing a red bikini and a lot of necklaces that all seem to be made of knotted leather. Her hair is long and so blond it's almost white. Willa pulls her in close by her bare hips, kisses her on the mouth. My goodness! It's so weird that the babies grow up one day and have sex all over the place. I look at my mother, who is politely looking the other way so as not to draw attention to everybody's inadvertent gayness.

"Grandma, Grandpa, this is my friend Callie," Willa says.

"Lovely to meet you, Callie," my mother says, and my father gives a kind of comedic salute from his chair.

"Oh, wait, and this is my mom. Mom, Callie. Callie, this is my mom, Rachel. Everybody mostly calls her Rocky."

"Hello, mysterious Callie of the late-night outings," I say, and Willa rolls her eyes like a fifth grader.

"Nice to meet you all," Callie says.

"That's my dad in the water," Willa says, pointing. "And my brother and his girlfriend." Callie nods.

"I can't really stay," Callie says, pointing up the beach.

"She's a lifeguard," Willa explains.

"Cool," I say. "Give us the insider info if there's, like, a riptide or sharks or anything."

"There *are* sharks," Callie says.

"Oh, I just mean, like, *imminently*," I say, and she nods, shrugs, says, "I mean, there are actually lots of sharks all the time, tbh."

"Yikes!" I say. "Well, please come and rescue us specifically if you see any."

"Will do," she says, laughing. She and Willa head up the beach, their perfect arms slung around each other.

"Your children are lovely," my mother says, and squeezes my hand. "Just lovely."

I hold her fingers in mine for an extra minute, feel them tremble, before she snatches her hand back to her own lap.

"You good?" I say, and she says, "Don't be silly. Of course."

"I am very invested in you being alive, Mom, as you know."

"I know, darling."

"So if there's something I should be worrying about, you need to tell me."

"I will. I promise." She's a liar, but I let myself be comforted anyway.

. . .

When we lost the baby—*lost the baby!* Like he fell out of a coat pocket on the bus—my parents sent flowers, sent Zabar's, offered to drive out and help. Jamie was four then. The next time, he was five. "I think we're okay," I said, which was not actually true. But it was enough to know they would. Just the love inside the offer. The grace of it.

There are some things I haven't told you yet—and will. And there are other things I won't. Willa, for example, has a story that's not mine to share. I'll just tell you that one spring morning three years ago I posted a photograph from a hospital window of a Boston park in bloom and a friend on social media—a person I had never even met in real life—wrote me privately to say, "Hey, I know that view. I'm here, head of pediatrics. Let me know if you need anything or if I can help in any way." I cried then. I am crying now, remembering. Despair laced through with so much incredible beauty. We just keep showing up for each other. Even through the mystery of other people's grief. What else is there?

My mother wants to walk up to the path along the dunes. She's spotted a handful of ripe rose hips. "Not enough for jelly, I don't think. But we could probably make a pot of tea." When I was a little girl, my mother taught me to bite into the mealy red fruit to gauge its readiness: you wanted to taste sugar on your tongue, even as your jaws were cramping from the tartness. "They didn't used to ripen until after the first frost," she says now, and I say only, "Weird," because why point out that the climate is changing? It's so dull and stressful. My mother wipes out a sandwich bag with the corner of her towel, stuffs it into her pocket, stands, reaches out her hands to help me up. This does not go well. I end up pulling her into my lap because she is the approximate size and weight of an elderly hummingbird, and then I end up pushing her over into the sand, where she lies in a crumpled ball, laughing. My dad looks over from his *New York Times* crossword puzzle, shakes his head, says, "Please try not to kill my wife," uncaps his pen again. Nick jogs up, seawater streaming from his hair, and rights my mom, stands her up on her sandaled feet. She thanks him and shakes herself off, takes my hand to trudge up into the sandy hills because if there is wild food being dished up by this glorious Cape Cod summer sunshine, what can we do but help ourselves?

17

Jamie was four then, and Willa was not yet one. We'd moved from Boston to Western Massachusetts earlier that year, and there wasn't a gynecologist I knew. When we got home from the Cape, I picked one on a friend's tepid recommendation: "He's kind of a douche, but he did okay delivering my babies. Sorry," she said. "That's all I got."

I lay bottomless on the table, in my T-shirt and socks, trying to feel like an actual person. The doctor stood over me, looked down at me. "The ultrasound will tell us how far along you are now," he said.

"Okay," I said. *I have a baby at home*, I didn't say. *Can I just close my eyes for a minute?*

He probed me roughly with a lubricated wand, like he'd zipped down in a spaceship to learn about female earthlings and their proclivities. On the screen, grainy footage zipped past in black and white, and then something. A little black puddle. "There," he said. The puddle winked closed, winked back open as he adjusted the probe. "That's the gestational sac, and—here we go." He shifted the probe again and a tiny dot pulsed on the screen. "See that flutter? We've got a heartbeat, Mom!" Mom!

Jesus. I cried a little bit. He measured something, said, "Six weeks."

"I love him so much," Nick said, pretend boo-hooing, when I handed him the printout of the inky blot. He was quoting a Coen brothers comedy.

"Can you please not?" I said.

"I'm sorry," he said. He wrapped his arms around me. "It's so exciting!" he said, but I wasn't convinced—either that it was exciting or that Nick was excited. "I like its . . ." He pointed to the printout. "Whatever this is."

"I think that's just lint," I said, and brushed it off.

"Oh!" he said. "Still." We heard Willa waking up from her nap, crying out to be nursed. I went to her where she lay on our futon. When she saw me, her face broke all the way open into a smile. She flipped over onto her stomach and used my sweatpants to pull herself to standing. I reached down to scoop her up, and she touched my face with one fat finger. Pure wonder, pure joy. "Mama!"

It was a month later that I begged Nick to drive me back to the ocean. September. "Please," I said. "One night on the Cape. I just need to swim."

"Of course," he said. "Anything you want."

I bled the baby away into the brine. There were no sharks that I could see. I wanted obliteration. But also, I wanted life. I wanted to keep the life I had.

18

The house is very, very full. I've had many excellent ideas in my life, but all of us staying here together might not have been one of them.

Between the outdoor shower and the indoor shower, everybody manages to get cleaned up, but there are seven of us and only a single sketchy toilet. Also there are damp beach towels and bath towels everywhere.

"Jamie, honey, can you please figure out a way to hang all these towels up outside?" He's happy to! He disappears onto the deck with a roll of kitchen twine and a couple of bungee cords—a kid, like his father, who loves a problem he can actually solve.

My mother is sweet-talking Chicken. "Who's a pretty cat?" she says to him rhetorically, and he blinks at her slowly, falls onto his side so he can knead his besotted paws in the air. "Is he supposed to be on the table?" she says, and I shrug.

"You're such a cat lover, Mom," I say to her. "You should get another one." There'd always been cats when I was growing up: tabbies, gingers, tuxedos. I'd dressed them in bonnets and sweater vests and hardly thought about the siblings I never had.

To be honest, though, I was lonely anyway. My parents loved me, but their great romance did not leave much empty space. Whose heart could I fill? And who could fill mine? I was an outlet with nothing plugged into it. Later they were mad at me for being a slutty teenager, but I just wanted what they had. Or something like it.

"I don't want your father to trip on a cat and break his hip," she says. Chicken is in her arms now, his head resting in the crook of her neck. "And besides, who will take care of a cat after we go?"

"Um, first of all, we will," I say. "And second of all, I'm pretty sure a cat isn't going to outlive you just yet."

"Don't be too sure," my dad complains from their bed. He's gone to lie down. "In related news, my sciatica is killing me. Can someone please bring me a glass of water and some Advil?" My mother hands me the cat and goes to him.

Maya is on the couch with her feet in Willa's lap. They're passing the free real-estate circular back and forth, guessing prices and screaming in occasional horror and disbelief. "*Asbestos remediation included!*—with an exclamation point. For two point six million dollars." Maya looks a little, as my mom would say, *green around the gills*, but I leave her alone. She and Jamie have been dating for forever now—since they were college students. Five years? Six? We love her. And still I don't know what she's thinking. How she's feeling. I imagine it might rack her nerves a little, keeping such a big secret around all of these noisy and complicated people who are almost like family but maybe not quite.

"Take this," I say, and hand Chicken to Willa, who *oof*s under his weight.

"Am I the slimmest cat you've ever known?" she asks in the cat's voice, and I say, "You are!" but then wink at Willa, because I'm lying. "He's so fat!" she whispers, as herself now, and lifts him like a barbell to kiss his tummy.

Nick arrives from a last-minute dinner run. He's picked up the corn and the fish, the tub of cocktail shrimp, the white wine my parents like. "You're a good egg, Nicky," I say. "Thank you." I'm cutting up tomatoes, and he nuzzles the back of my neck, feels me up while he's unloading crackers into the cabinet above me. Oh, I do love to be wanted!

Maya pushes open the slider to join Jamie on the deck, where all the towels are now draped and gently flapping like a giant's prayer flag. I hear them laughing, see them bent over something. I catch Willa's eye and she pantomimes smoking a joint. "You're making a face like a grimace emoji," she says.

"I think it's just called *grimacing*," I say.

"What is that dreadful smell?" my mother says now. She is standing in the doorway of the bedroom, nose to the air like a school principal at 4:20. Maya and Jamie have wisely disappeared from the deck and into the woods beyond.

"Skunk?" Willa says, and my mother says, "Maybe. It smells a bit like marijuana. Now that it's legal in New York you can't walk one block without whacking great clouds of it wafting everywhere. It makes me positively *gag*!"

"Drama queen," Willa says, and pats the couch next to her. "Come sit with me, Grandma. Give your poor offended nose a rest. Look at the outrageous Cape Cod listings because maybe you wanted to buy a literal shack for three-quarters of a million dollars."

My mother does as she's told. "Do I like *marsh views*?" I hear her ask my daughter, and Willa says, "Only if you like marsh *smells*. Picture garbage, but made out of crabs."

"Oh dear, no!" she says, and then, "Rachel, shall I start putting out the appetizers?"

"Please!" I say.

Willa hoists my mother to her feet, and she walks the five steps to the refrigerator, gathers cheese and cocktail sauce and lemons, takes everything outside. Nick brings her the shrimp, a box of crackers, a container of green olives, a platter, and a knife, and my mother sits at the patio table to cut lemons into wedges and arrange everything. Meanwhile my father has emerged, and he sits down next to Willa with a big sigh. Willa asks after his nap, which was *perfect, absolutely perfect*. The cat hops up into his lap, and my father pats his head roughly like he's a dog, which makes Chicken flatten his ears in addled pleasure. The big kids return to the deck, and I hear my mother swatting them away from the shrimp she's trying to arrange.

"Can you stop cooking and have a glass of wine with us?" my father asks, managing to host me even though I'm supposed to be hosting him. I can! I turn the burner to low under the corn pot, put the fish in the fridge, wipe my hands on a dish towel, and join them. We pull chairs around, pour pinot grigio, distribute napkins and little plates.

Willa declines a glass of wine. "I like to act sophisticated," she says, "but in truth I'm kind of a teeto-taller." Everybody looks at her. "That's not how that word's pronounced," she guesses, and I say, "It's not," and she laughs. "I think I've only ever seen it in writing."

"Grandpa, can you tell us more about your family?" Willa

asks my dad. She's nibbling an olive pit. She's recently done one of those mail-away DNA tests and has become very interested in her ancestry. According to her results, I am sixty-one percent Ashkenazi Jew, which leaves a baffling eleven percent on my mother's side. "Someone fucked a Jew—but who?" Willa said, and her grandmother tutted at her and said, "Don't be crude, Willa." "But seriously," Willa said. "It's kind of hard to picture." It really was! All of them planting pansies and eating lemon drizzle cake and waving to the queen—a secret Jew among them. Meanwhile, she's curious about my dad too.

"Tell us a little more about Poland," she says to him now.

My father absentmindedly plucks a cracker shard off his lap, puts it in his mouth. "What is it you want to know about Poland?"

"I guess I don't totally understand when your parents came to the United States," she says. "I mean, I know your mother came from Russia—Ukraine—in the nineteen twenties. But when did your father's family come?" This was my own grandfather, a belligerent pastrami-scented man who sold ribbon and beads in the garment district and died of a heart attack before my kids were born.

"He came in the twenties too," my dad explains. "They sent him over with his two sisters. Just the three kids on a boat to Ellis Island. It took two months. They got lice, I know. They were afraid it would get them sent back."

"They must have been terrified," Willa says, wide-eyed with imagining.

My father nods, bites a shrimp out of its tail, chews and swallows, takes a big sip of his wine. "They were, I'm sure. I mean, he didn't really talk about it. But of course. You can probably look them up, actually. I think Ellis Island has all the records." Willa will.

"They lived with relatives in Brooklyn?" Jamie asks, and my father nods. This is the part of the story my kids know: that the parents were supposed to join them there, but never saved enough money to come.

"And you never met your grandparents on your father's side?" Willa asks.

"That's right. I was born in 1935. And my grandparents died in Poland in 1942."

"The same year as each other?" Willa says, and my father says, "Of course."

"Why *of course*?" I say.

He blinks. "At Treblinka."

"The village near Warsaw," I clarify for the kids. "He doesn't mean the camp."

My father looks at me and raises his bushy white eyebrows, shakes his head.

"Mort," my mother says, like a warning.

"Dad," I say. My arms prickle with goose bumps.

Willa bursts into tears, says, "Sorry. I'm sorry. I don't understand what is happening." My father pats her back.

"I am not trying to cause a problem here. But yes, Treblinka, the extermination camp. Rocky, you know this."

"Dad, no. I don't."

"How do you not know this?"

I'm crying a little bit too now. "I mean, I really have no idea. I guess I don't know because nobody ever told me. Although I definitely asked. I asked more than once. Did you"—it's not

going to be the right word, but I can't think of a better one—
"*lie* to me?"

"Lie? No. I don't think it was a lie. Not exactly. And besides,
you must have wanted to believe it. You're not stupid, Rachel.
How did you imagine two Jews died in occupied Poland under
Hitler?"

"Don't *scold* me!" I say. "*Nobody knew how they died*. I'm
pretty sure that's what you told me. So don't keep a huge, terrible secret from me and then be mad at me that I don't know it!"

Nick pushes his chair back to stand up, comes to wrap his
arms around me from behind. My mother and Willa are pat-
ting me from opposite sides. I am lousy with comfort. I am also
trapped and having a massive hot flash.

"It wasn't a secret," my father says, and shrugs.

"I think," I say, and then stop. I'm so sad and angry that
I feel like my sweating skull is going to break open like a
grief piñata, my terrible feelings raining down on everyone. "I
think," I say again, "that it was precisely a secret. I spent my
entire childhood reading books about the Holocaust, Dad. You
know that."

My father shrugs again, drags a shrimp through the cocktail sauce, says, "It is what it is."

"*What?*" I say. My mother digs in her pocket and passes me
a tissue, hooks her bony little arm through mine. "What does
that even mean? *It is what it is?*"

"Hey, Mama?" This is Willa, gentle. "This is a lot. It's so,
so much. But I wonder if you want to shift gears? Grandpa is
telling you something about—about himself, really. More than
he's telling you something about *you*, I think."

"Thanks, honey," I say, and Jamie smiles, says, "Did you just low-key roast Mama for being a narcissist?" I love these kids more every day.

"I'm sorry, Dad," I say. "I'm so sorry. What a trauma—to grow up with so much pain in the house." In his house. In everybody's house. My god. All the motherless children. All the childless mothers. A canyon the size of a continent, and full of bones. "I can't even imagine," I say. "Forgive me." I reach a hand across the table to him.

"No," my dad says. He takes my hand. "I'm the one who should be sorry. I never meant it to be a secret. But I see that it was. I don't understand how so much time has passed. How I'm so old, and there are still things you don't know. I've always meant to tell you, but I just"—he hesitates—"haven't. I didn't."

"You have now," I say. "Tell us more. Can you?"

"I will," he says. "I would like that. But maybe not now. I'm tired, and there's the fish."

"Of course," I say. "Let me make dinner."

Hours later, the candles have burned down on their plates into pools of translucent wax. The sun has set, the mosquitoes have come and gone, and our dishes are pushed away. I ended up pan-roasting the striper and served it with a caper-lemon-butter sauce. It was perfect. The corn was burstingly sweet, the star pasta simple and good, the tomatoes bright and restorative. Nick has opened a second bottle of wine. A third. Maya has pulled the bed out in the living room, and she and Jamie are lying down in the lamplight. Now it's just my parents, Nick, Willa, and me outside still. Talking some, laughing, picking at the good chocolate bar I've broken into pieces. I am full to bursting in every way.

"We didn't hear from them," my dad is explaining, about his grandparents. "Some people we knew got letters from friends or relatives saying, 'We're being deported,' or, 'They're rounding up the neighborhood.' We didn't hear anything at all. A holiday card one year, and then boom, nothing. Silence." He shakes his head. "My aunts would come over and my brother—your uncle Sal—and I would eavesdrop. We were just kids, remember. We didn't really understand what we were hearing, and nobody thought it was appropriate to explain it to us. We listened to the conversations, to the radio. We tried to piece it together."

"That must have been so confusing, Grandpa," Willa says, and he nods.

"It was. But we were kids. We wanted to play stickball. Broomball. We all got metal roller skates and we wanted to roller-skate around the streets, buy a hot dog from the hot dog guy. It wasn't just one thing."

I picture my dad and uncle in their one-bedroom apartment on the Lower East Side, trying to listen to the grown-ups talking. Trying not to. Maybe this is what I did too.

Willa dips her fingertips into the melted wax, peels it off and rolls it up, pokes it back into the candle to melt again. The candlelight illuminates her apple cheeks. I think, *My baby!* and keep this thought to myself.

"Do you know when your family knew for sure?" she asks. My father nods.

"I think—and I may be wrong about this—but I think we got a letter in 1944. Maybe 1945, though I'm pretty sure it was before the end of the war. From Warsaw neighbors of theirs who'd been deported to Siberia. I think—and again, I'm not sure—but I think they'd seen my grandparents get put on a freight car. Though why wouldn't the neighbors have been rounded up then too? I'm not sure. I might be confused about this."

"Did your parents read you the letter?" This is my mom asking. I note that she, also, seems not to know this whole story, which I find strangely reassuring.

"No, no," my dad says. "I don't know how we heard about it. Probably we just overheard it. I remember, though, that my father cried out. A sound I'd never heard him make. I never heard it again." This sounds so much like a picture book we used to read the kids—one about an old couple reuniting decades after the Holocaust—that I wonder if it's true.

"We never spoke of it," my dad says.

"You mean you never talked about your grandparents, Grandpa? Or about the Holocaust?"

"Either, really," my dad says. "Everyone was so—I don't know. Sad, of course. But also there was so much guilt. Shame maybe, even. That they had survived personally. But also— and this is just me looking back now—that this had happened to us at all, as Jews. This monstrous thing! How had we let it? What kind of people were we? It was preposterous."

"Is that what all the Jewish guilt is?" I say. For some reason this has never occurred to me. "I mean, if I went back in time— were we less guilty, like, as a *people*, before the Holocaust?"

"I doubt it," my dad says. "Living Jews are always the survivors. That goes way back."

"Back before the camps," Willa says.

"Back before the camps," my dad echoes.

"Do you think that's why you hated summer camp?" Willa says to me. "Because of the word *camp*?"

"No, honey. I hated it because Grandma and Grandpa sent me to *Lord of the Flies* camp, and everyone threw dodgeballs at your head and gave you impetigo. But that's an interesting thought." *Camp*. Jesus.

Willa laughs, grows serious again. In the silence, the crickets are scraping out their ancient songs. "You must have felt so haunted, Grandpa, growing up with that in the house," she says.

"Haunted?" he says. "I don't think I'd go that far. It was a sad thing, sure. But we had enough to eat. We were safe— relatively safe. We lived our lives." He shrugs. "What else can you do?"

"I don't know," I say, even though I'm thinking about myself again—about inherited trauma. "I mean, that's great, I guess. But I don't know."

"*I* know," my father says. "It is a privilege to grow old. We are lucky to be here."

"We really are," my mother says. I cry a little then, because of the conversation and the wine and this absolute devastation and blessedness, rolled up into a lump in my own throat that I have been trying to swallow for my whole life.

Life is a seesaw, and I am standing dead center, still and balanced: living kids on one side, living parents on the other. Nicky here with me at the fulcrum. *Don't move a muscle*, I think. But I will, of course. You have to.

19

The summer Jamie was five and Willa was not yet two, Nick and I went back to the OB for our follow-up appointment. We'd already seen the heartbeat. We'd magneted the grainy printout to the fridge. I had a secret note taped under my desk with the names *Boris* and *Pearl* written on it. It's still there—*like an amulet*, I want to say, but what is there to ward off now? In the exam room, the nurses weighed me and stretched a tape measure over the slight bulge of my stomach. "Thirteen weeks," the doctor said when he came in. He was nicer to me with Nick there. "Let's see what we can see."

"I want to hear the little hoofbeat heartbeat," I said. "I could already feel Willa kicking at this point. I just want more"—what?—"contact," I said. But what I meant was *proof.*

"Unlikely," the doctor said. "That you could feel movement at thirteen weeks." He was already pushing the transducer into the side of my stomach. I hated him.

"Careful," I said, urologically. "I have a full bladder." Nick reached out from his chair for my hand.

"Here we go," the doctor said. He pressed harder. "Almost had it. Hang on." The grainy footage zipped past, and then the baby was there—that sweet little curl of a sea creature. I could see the profile of her face. I could see her stillness—could feel, in my belly, the stillness I was seeing on the screen.

And suddenly I knew. Maybe I'd known already.

"Just locating the heartbeat," he said, but I was crying.

"No," I said. "No, no, no."

"Hang on, hang on. Relax, Mom. You're making it more difficult." He squeezed more gel onto my stomach.

"No," I said. He pressed hard, peered into the screen, put the probe down, and left the room.

"Nicky," I said, and he stood then, squatted down by me.

"It's okay," he said. "It's probably fine. This probably happens all the time."

"No," I said. "Oh, no. That poor little thing."

More people came into the room then in their white coats, pointed at the screen, spoke among themselves, shook their heads, confirmed the worst. I felt like a bad stork who'd dropped its precious bundle mid-flight.

They ran down the options for us: D&C—the surgical and immediate "solution." Medication, like misoprostol, to "get things going." And what they called the "wait and see" approach—which seemed to suggest that there were multiple outcomes, when really there was just the one: wait and see the blood that means you're not having a baby, which you already know. Every word they chose enraged me, every so-called *option*, as if I were selecting dinner from a restaurant menu. *Do you want to lose the baby? Or would you prefer losing the baby?* The thought of them sticking any more things into me was unendurable. And waiting sounded like torture. I picked the medication.

"We're supposed to go on vacation next week," I said. "Can I still swim in the ocean?"

"It's probably not a good idea," they said.

"Why not?" I said. "The baby's already dead."

They exchanged uneasy glances. Was I supposed to be more delicate? Jesus fucking Christ.

"It's probably just best not to," they said.

I looked at the handout. I was still lying on my side on the table. "No swimming in lakes or rivers," I read. "It doesn't say anything about the ocean."

"Okay," my own doctor said. "If that's a risk you want to take, you can."

I sat up, then, so that I could get dressed and leave before I actually murdered somebody.

I closed my eyes in the car, put a hand on my belly inside of which was our stilled child—a withered little peach, the blush off its cheeks. There was something in my brain like a dial tone, and I wondered if I would die. But I wouldn't, of course. I'd get home and boil noodles like every grieving mother everywhere.

Later, I lay in bed reading the leaflet that came from the pharmacy. "Expulsion of fecal matter," I read aloud to Nick. "Ew. That's all we need."

He looked over, said, "*Fetal*, honey," and I said, "Oh, that's better, I guess," and turned off my lamp.

The kids were asleep in a little tumble between us. We hadn't really bothered trying to get them out of our bed at that point. They were small. They smelled good. They craved our company. I looked at Willa's dark crescent of eyelashes, her cheek pearly in the moonlight filtering through our bedroom window. Jamie's pink little mouth with a thumb in it. I'd only ever wanted two kids—that was the truth. But the body wanted more. *My* body, I guess I should say. Though, wow, it sure didn't feel like mine.

THURSDAY

20

"How the hell do you do this? Alice, what the hell?"

I wake to the sound of my father wrestling with the Nespresso. It's hissing and steaming and he's cursing at it.

"This is plain water. Where does the coffee come out? Jesus Christ."

"Mort, here, let me. You have to put one of these things in somewhere. Stop. Mort, give me that. Sit *down*. I'll do it."

"Jesus Christ," my father says again.

I peer out of the loft and see Jamie and Maya holding pillows over their heads.

"You guys," I call down to the kids. "Go lie down in Grandma and Grandpa's bed. I'm sure they're not going back to sleep." They rise and stumble off, greeting the grandparents on their way.

"I'm sorry, darling!" my mother calls up. "Did your father wake you? He's dreadfully noisy."

"Oh, it's totally fine!" I say. "I was going to get up anyway."

Willa, who did not see her friend as planned last night—we don't know why—is asleep on the inflatable mattress next to my side of the bed. This is a familiar sight from the many, many years of her sleeping by me. She used to drag her little futon into our room in the night, angry and insulted to have woken and found herself alone. Then she would carry in all her dolls and stuffed animals, arrange them on the little mattress—the *crouton*, we called it—and climb up into bed with us. "You losed me," she would say directly into my face, pressing her cold, furious hands and feet under my T-shirt to warm them on my stomach. "And I'm the smallest one. Why you losed me when I was sleeping?" I could see her tiny little seed-pearl teeth shining in the dark. "I'm so glad you're found," I would say. "Because here you are!" I was always happy to see her. It's true that I didn't want to sit on the floor in the afternoon and play with trains or pour imaginary tea. But I was a good parent in the night.

Chicken, asleep on the small of Willa's back, swooshes his tail and blinks lovingly when I smile at him. The fact that he is not downstairs begging for his breakfast is evidence of how fully chaotic my parents are.

"What the hell kind of toaster is this?" my father is saying now. "Why do I have to turn so many knobs? Dark? Light? Bake? Broil? I can't just make toast? It has to be rocket science?"

"Mort," my mother says. "Mort, sit down. You're going to burn yourself. This is the exact same toaster oven we have at home."

"Is it?" my dad says, abashed. "Oh."

"Oh my god," I whisper, and Nick, curled up next to me with his eyes closed, laughs. He pushes a hand up under my T-shirt to cup one of my breasts, and I push him off, kiss him, slide down to the bottom of the bed so I can stand without stepping on our daughter. I mince down the spiral staircase in my memory-foam slippers, all of my joints clacking like the witch in a marionette performance of *Hansel and Gretel*.

"Good morning!" I say to my beautiful parents who are also, somehow, these stooped and white-haired old people. They greet me cheerfully and I brush my teeth with the door open so I can listen to them Goldilocks around, looking for a pan to scramble some eggs in: too big, too small, too nonstick, not nonstick enough.

"Let me poach you an egg, darling," my mother says, and my dad says, "Oh! That would be wonderful! Thank you."

Nick comes down and, bless him, remakes the sofa so my dad can go and sit down. I heat milk in the microwave and make coffee for my parents. I make some for Nick and me too, ice it. It's already hot and promises to get hotter.

Like a church bell chiming the sick hour, the bedroom door pops open and Maya rushes into the bathroom, tugs the door closed behind her. I try to talk loudly to my mother, but I see her craning an ear toward the muddled sounds of water and gagging. Even though she doesn't hear that well, this is the kind of thing she never misses.

"Oh dear," she says, and I say, "Yeah, it's okay. She's been having some gastric issues. She's going to check it out when she gets back to New York. Maybe a food allergy of some kind. I'm sure she's fine."

Maya waves shyly on her way out of the bathroom, creeps back into the bedroom, and pulls the door closed behind her.

"Such a lovely girl," my mother says.

"I know," I say. "She's perfect."

. . .

Nick has gone out for a *paper* paper, and the four of us pass sections around on the shady deck while the kids finish sleeping. We interrupt each other's silent reading constantly, noisily sharing from our own articles about politics, luggage tags, Covid, flan.

"Why would we elect this guy?" my dad is saying about a particular political candidate. "He's basically a hobo."

"Dad, you really can't say *hobo* anymore," I say.

"*Hobo,*" my dad says.

"Right. You can't really say that."

"Oh," he says. "I thought you thought I said *homo*."

On our phones we do the Wordle, the Spelling Bee. Nick finishes everything first, and the rest of us rail against his relaxed competence and, while we're at it, his relentless good nature.

"Have you ever been angry, Nick?" my dad asks him. "I've known you for—what?—thirty years, and I don't think I've ever seen you angry."

"I've seen him angry," I say. "I've *made* him angry."

"Well, you're the right tool for that job," my dad says, which is accurate.

"It's true that anger is not typically my first response," Nick says affably. We wait to see if he's going to say anything else, but he is back to his phone.

"He's playing online Scrabble with Luca," I explain to my parents. "My old boyfriend."

"I haven't thought of Luca in ages!" my mother says. "How is he?"

"I don't actually know," I say.

"He's good," Nick says. "He and his wife just bought a house in Connecticut."

"I always liked Luca," my father says, trying to catch Nick's eye. We call this particular pattern of behavior *shit-disturbing*. It has much in common with picking at a scab because you're bored. Sometimes the scab peels off and the wound beneath bleeds and you wish you were a different kind of person. Other times, like now, the scab refuses to budge.

"I bet you did," Nick says sincerely, without looking up. "Luca's the best."

"That was disappointing for you," I say to my dad, and he laughs.

Nick's own parents are difficult in very different ways from mine. His mother, for example, does not track Nick's life or the lives of our children. When the kids were little, she sent birthday cards with the wrong ages on them: A lion holding a 3-shaped balloon the year Willa turned five; a clown announcing, "You're ten!" when Jamie was thirteen. Now she sends cards at fully random times of the year, and they always say the same thing: "You are wished a happy birthday." "By whom, though?" we all like to say, because we're assholes. "Oh, you can be a dick about my mom," Nick always reassures all of us. "She's the worst." What she is, among other things, is a pill addict. A person with a substance-use disorder. Nick's dad compensates by sending us occasional wads of cash in the mail. Two hundred dollars in tens; eighty-five dollars in ones and fives.

"Your father has a checking account," I always say. "Can't he use it? Cash in the mail is so nerve-racking to me."

"It really makes no difference," Nick says, which is kind of true. "We'll get the money or someone else will. We have enough. It's fine." Okay, Dalai Lama!

We fly to Florida once a year to visit. The house smells like cat pee and cigarettes, and the TV is always on.

"You're just a snob," Willa said to me once when I complained about having to go. "I mean, that's fair. It's not really your fault. But that is what we're talking about. Classism, basically."

"I notice you're not actually coming with us, though," I said. We'd planned the trip to coincide with Willa's spring break.

"Busted," she said, and laughed. "I guess I just hate being there? But they're kind of homophobes, though, so it's a little more legit."

A year after she graduated from high school, they'd sent her a congratulatory beige purse with a pair of nude pantyhose tucked inside. "This will be very useful for my new life as a corporate femme!" she'd joked. "Although I will admit the color *nude* is kind of exciting. Just conceptually."

"Oh no!" my mother says. She points to the screen door, against which Chicken is pressing himself so desperately that you expect his head to push through like a sieved egg. "It's getting a bit sunny anyway," she says, gathering up the breakfast dishes. "I'm going to go in and think about putting on my bathing suit. Give that poor pussycat a little attention."

The kids are up, scattered around and quietly eating bowls of colorful cereal. Chicken is running around now, banging his face up into their bowls in the hopes that they'll spill milk for him to lap up, a behavior that Willa calls Goat-butt Head and scolds him for.

"But why I can't have any cereal?" she says in his voice, and then, when nobody answers, she says, "Because you're a bad cat," in her own.

I tear off seven pieces of tinfoil and start making my sandwich inquiries. "Who wants what?" I say. "There's turkey, ham, Swiss, American, and all the extras—mustard, mayo, pickles, pickled peppers. Lettuce, tomato, cukes. I'm happy to make tuna. There's hummus too, actually. Coleslaw. There's even a little bit of leftover striper."

"Is there mortadella?" my dad says.

"There's not," I say.

"Hmm," he says. "Is there salami?"

"I thought you didn't eat salami because of the garlic," I say, and he shrugs, says, "Sometimes I do. Today I would."

"Mort," my mother says. "Don't be a pain. There's turkey, ham, and cheese."

"No condiments?" my dad says.

I am reminded of waitressing—of the kind of large table where every single person, one after the other, asks you to list all the salad dressings. *Italian, Light Italian, Thousand Island, Ranch, Blue Cheese, Balsamic Vinaigrette, Honey-Mustard Vinaigrette.* "Wait. What are they again? Is there Catalina French?" I met Nick at that job. "Tell me the salad dressings," he whispered to me, in bed.

"That's right, no condiments," I say now, and my dad looks at me, says, "Ah, you're kidding. Okay. Sorry. I'm old! It's not a crime to be deaf. I want the usual condiments. Just regular ones—nothing hokey."

"Okay," I say.

"I don't need my lunch festooned with figs and seeds," my dad continues, and I say, "Dad. I got it."

"Okay," he says. "I'm just trying to make myself clear."

"Thank you," I say. "Because I was maybe going to festoon your lunch with figs and seeds."

"Testy," he observes, which is true.

"Is this somebody's hairband?" my mother says, and I turn around when I hear Willa laughing. "Is that your hairband, Mom?" Willa says to me, pointing, and I can see that what my mom is holding is the silky sliver of a mauve thong. "Oh, Mom," I say. "I think that's probably Maya's. I think it might actually be underpants."

"It couldn't possibly be underpants!" my mother says, turning it over in her hands to look closer. "Maybe it's a headband. I'll just leave it here." She puts it on the table, and Willa actually chokes with laughter and goes upstairs.

I make lunch while everybody waits for a turn to use the bathroom. Once the cooler is packed up, I pull on my swimsuit and rub white sunscreen on my white arms and legs. I have a special little tube I use for my face, on account of my wrinkles and acne. Willa picks it up, reads the label.

"This is not even mineral sunscreen," she says. "It's full of all the toxins you tell us not to use. You're such a hypocrite!"

I sigh, say, "I make an exception. I just use a little. Plus, it makes my skin look great."

"Um, yeah, it makes your skin look great because it's makeup."

"It's not makeup!" I say. "It's just tinted sunscreen. Look. SPF fifty."

"Oooh, sorry, but no. It says here that it's *foundation*."

"Oh my god! No wonder it makes my skin look good." I

take the tube out of her hands. "It *is* foundation! Why do I feel so humiliated?"

"Because you like to think you're not the kind of person who wears makeup," Willa says. "It ruins the idea you have about yourself."

"That's exactly why," I say sadly.

I have had many ideas about myself—and many of them have been ruined. I do not share this thought with my daughter.

The summer Jamie was five and Willa was not yet two, Nick and I stopped at the pharmacy on the way home from the ultrasound. The doctor had called in the prescription, and I went to the pickup window to sign for it. I was crying on and off still, and Nick kept his arm around my waist.

"Do you have any questions about this medication?" the pharmacist asked. He looked at the computer screen in front of him. "Misoprostol. Oh, you've taken this before."

"No I haven't," I said, automatically.

"No, you have. It looks like . . ." He peered at the screen. "September of last year."

I felt Nick beside me, but I couldn't tell if he was paying attention or not.

"That must be a computer error," I said, and signed my name on the screen.

"Weird," Nick said in the car. "You like to think they keep track of stuff better than that."

I nodded, swallowed the pills with the end of somebody's coffee, and waited for exactly what I knew was coming.

It's one o'clock exactly, and we're waiting for the tram to the beach. "Herding cats" is the expression that pops into my head. Getting everyone into the cars, through the parking lot, and onto the tram line is like a sociological experiment about complaining. Or maybe it's like a religious experiment about Jews.

"You really can't say *Jews* and *experiment* in the same sentence, Mom," Willa says quietly. I hadn't realized I'd said this out loud.

"We do seem to have a critical mass of Jews here," I say, looking at the tram line.

"A *very* critical mass," Nick says quietly, and I laugh.

The tram arrives just as my dad suggests that we've been waiting all day. I look at my watch. It's 1:01.

"You just put all this stuff back here?" my dad says, watching me and Nick load all our chairs and bags and coolers and umbrellas into the open storage area in the back of the tram. "What if somebody steals it?"

"Dad, the tram ride is, like, one minute long. We'll get right out and grab the stuff. Nobody's going to steal it."

"I'm just saying," my dad says. "All those lovely sandwiches. Plus, my book."

"I'm pretty sure they sell John Grisham on the Cape," I say. I take his hand. "Just please get on the tram, Dad."

On the tram, Willa grills me about the four Hogwarts houses in the *Harry Potter* books. "Don't help her," she says to everyone. "Go."

All the names of everything have oozed out and away from the drainage holes menopause has punched into my memory storage.

"Dumbledore," I say, and Willa laughs.

"Good, Mom. Dumbledore."

"No, no," I say. "Not Dumbledore. Jesus. I read these books to you, like, eleventy zillion times. *Dumbledore?*"

"Still not Dumbledore," Willa says.

"Whiffenpoofs?" I say.

"Yup," she says, laughing.

"Snivelin? Weaslyton? Fuck."

"You got them all," she says. She is laughing so hard she's crying. "Good job."

At the entryway to the beach my mother points to the purple shark flag, alarmed. "I think they pretty much leave that up at this point," Maya says. "Climate change, warming waters, etcetera. It's suboptimal, definitely."

"Yikes," my mother says.

"Don't get too exercised about it, Alice," my father says. "When was the last time you went in the ocean?"

"Nineteen seventy-seven?" my mother says. "Still, I'd prefer the children not be eaten."

"Same," I say.

On the board where they tell you about the tides and the temperatures, there's a flyer for the Stroke Clinic. "Swim lessons," I clarify, after my father pantomimes a cerebrovascular attack. They write a riddle here every day too. Today's is something about teeth and a whale, and the punch line is *orcadontist*. "Jesus," my father says, shaking his head. "That's terrible."

Now he's telling me something about an old friend of theirs, but I'm distracted by the umbrella I'm trying to unfurl in the hot wind.

"He has rogues disease," he says.

"Rogues disease?" I say.

"Yeah. Rogues disease."

"Huh," I say. "I don't think I know what that is. Is he very sick?"

"Eh," my dad says. "It comes and goes. He can't eat a bran muffin."

"That doesn't sound overly constraining," I say. I turn the crank one time too many, and the umbrella flips inside out.

"No," my dad says. "Shit. Not rogues disease. Alice, what the hell does Lester have?"

"*Roans* disease," my mother says crisply.

"Roans?" I say. "With an *R*?" and she says, "Yes."

"*Crohn's* disease?" I say, and she says, "Yes."

"*Crone's* disease?" Willa says, and "Like what you have, Mama, ha ha ha!"

"Crohn's," I say, "with an *h*. It's a gut thing."

"Poor Lester," Willa says.

"He's okay," my mother says dismissively. "Rachel, I'm worried about your legs."

"Me too, Mom," I say, and she laughs, says, "No, the sun. Did you put sunscreen on them? Here, use mine."

"Oh my god, you're just like *my* mom!" Willa says to her. "You guys are so proprietary about us. Like, *I made your whole body from scratch—the least you can do is put some lip balm on it.*"

My mother holds out the tube of sunscreen and I take it from her so as not to exercise the other obvious option, which is acting like a belligerent child. Somebody's Frisbee lands in the sand at my feet, and an embarrassed tweenager darts up and grabs it and darts away. The breeze picks up a little spray from the ocean, sifts it over us. The sky is relentlessly blue with a hot white sun right in the middle of it. I pull a stack of Oreos from the bag and pass them to Willa, who is holding out her hand. I pull out another stack for myself. My parents decline. A seagull runs over to cock its head at us about the cookies.

"If seagulls were eagles, would we be more excited about them?" Willa asks.

"Say more?" I say.

"I mean, if they were special. I always feel so bad for the unspecial birds. The way we're always like, *Look! It's a beautiful majestic hawk!* And then we're like, *Oh, wait, forget it, it's just a stupid ugly turkey vulture.*"

"I know what you mean," I say.

"Turkey vultures do eat roadkill," my mother interjects, "which is helpful."

"I'm going to put my feet in the water," my dad says, hauling himself up to standing. "Please do not take photographs of me and put them on Google. I prefer not to be featured as a comedic stock character in the ongoing display of your life."

"Geez, Dad," I say. "Noted."

"I'll take them," Willa says to me, pointing. "I mean, look at how cute he is in his—what does he call them?—*trunks*."

"Don't you want to swim?" I ask her, and she frowns, says, "I get so cold now. I miss my brown fat." Ever since we learned that kids grow out of their special insulating layer, Willa's complained that she's freezing.

I can see Nick, Jamie, and Maya beckoning to my dad from the waves, but he shakes his head, stays ankle-deep. Thank god. My ancient father actually swimming in the ocean feels like a bridge too far in terms of what I can handle fretting about. The *Jaws* soundtrack plays in my head forebodingly enough as it is.

"Drink some water, Grandma," I hear Willa say. "It's really hot out."

"Yes, darling," my mother says.

The summer Jamie was four and Willa was not yet one, I lay on the beach inside a shade tent we'd set up for her nap. I felt like a sultan. I felt like a prisoner. Jamie darted up from the shoreline to peer in at us. "Are you coming out?" he whispered.

"Should we leave Willa here all by herself?" I said. "She is a pretty big girl."

Jamie laughed. "Can I come in?" he whispered, and I said, "Of course." He slid himself—sandy legs, hot torso, wet swimsuit—between the baby and me. I was so tired. "Where's Daddy?" I said, and he shrugged. He was probably swimming. His persistent carefreeness enraged me. "I feel so trapped all the time," I'd said to him that morning. "I feel like I'm going to gnaw your leg off." "I think," he'd said, smiling, "that the expression is about gnawing off one's *own* leg." "Whatever," I'd said.

"Is this the ocean?" Jamie whispered.

"It is," I said. "It's the Atlantic Ocean."

"So I can just pee right here?"

"Oh! Honey. No." I had misunderstood the question. "No. Inside the tent isn't the ocean. Just the water is. Do you need to pee?"

"No," he said. "I was just wondering if I *did* need to pee. And there's no pooping, Mama, right? Not even in the watery part of the ocean. I know that now."

He was studying me with his big brown eyes. Eyes, nose, mouth. The children's features shattered me a little bit—as if someone had siphoned love out of me and tattooed it onto someone else's face.

"I'm just closing my eyes for a sec, honey. Pat Willa back to sleep if she wakes up," I said, and Jamie said, "Okay, Mama." It was one thousand degrees and a greenfly was buzzing around us and, within my own swimsuit, my breasts ached. I was starving. I was pregnant. I was sick and thirsty. I was gutted with love for these sparkling children. Bodies of my body. Inside and out—brain, heart, uterus; mouth, skin, breasts—not a single part of me was my own.

I doze a little in the shade now, the *New Yorker* stuck to my lap, and when I open my eyes, Jamie is squatting next to my chair, looking at me.

"What's up, pussycat?" I say, and he smiles, says, "Want to take a walk with me, Mom?" Uh-oh. I grab my hat.

This is a kid who likes drama and conflict about as much as his dad does—which is to say, not at all. He does not rage or scold. He says only, as we head up the beach, "I wish you would've not been the person she told first."

"I'm really sorry," I say. I stop walking so I can look at him—his hazel eyes and lean jaw and the impossible scruff of his two-day beard. Body of my body. "I understand why you're upset."

"I am," he says calmly. "I feel like this has pretty much nothing to do with you, but still, somehow, you're in the middle of it."

"Oof," I say.

"That was harsh," he says. "I'm sorry."

"No," I say. "Don't be. You're right."

He shrugs apologetically.

"People like talking to you, which is not a thing you're doing wrong," he says.

"But my boundaries are bad," I say. "I'm sorry."

"That's okay," he says. "It's the flip side of something I appreciate about you."

"I'm totally not done talking about you being mad at me," I say. "I'm here for it. But do you want to also talk about your girlfriend being pregnant?"

"I think not with you," he says gently. Then he sighs. "I mean, annoyingly, I do actually want to talk to you about it. But I also want to be a grown-up."

"I think you can do both," I say. "But I'm biased."

"It's her call, obviously," he says. "I'm one hundred percent down with whatever she wants to do. I think she understands that. I'm trying not to even form an opinion yet."

"You're a good one," I say and hug him, even though he's a foot taller than I am and the pressing of my old-lady boobs into his stomach probably gives him a massive case of the willies. "You guys will be great, whatever you do."

• • •

"We could *not* have it," I said to Nick, that shade-tent summer.

He raised his eyebrows. "Your call," he said. "Obviously."

"But you want to?" I said, and he said, "I mean, yeah. I don't think we have an especially compelling reason *not* to."

I felt like a person being sent back to class from the nurse's office—*You seem fine!*—even though I was holding my own bloody heart in my hands.

Jamie and I turn around to walk back down the beach and we can see that there's a crowd on the shore, everybody pointing to the water. Oh my god! "Grandpa is drowning!" I cry, and Jamie says, "What? Mom, wait!" But I am running.

23

My father is *not* drowning—as evidenced by the fact of him standing there on the shore in his dry trunks.

"Dad," I say. I'm breathless.

"There's a shark!" he says. He's pointing, excited. "I didn't see it, but Mom did. The lifeguards yelled everybody out of the water with a bullhorn. Willa's friend came."

"I thought you were drowning!" I say.

"Why would I be drowning?" he says. "Then again, why wouldn't I be?"

"Wow!" Jamie says. "I'm sorry we missed the shark!"

"They saw a fin and maybe blood?" my dad says. "There was a seal, I think. I don't actually know. I can't see anything. Or hear, really."

A drone is flying around over our heads, and everybody around us is still pointing and talking. A lifeguard walks importantly past us in his red swimsuit, even though he's, like, ten years old. It seems that there is no longer a shark to be seen, but it's always unsettling to be reminded that the ocean is full of them.

• • •

But the shark is a red herring, because Jamie touches my shoulder, points, and there's another crowd gathering where our stuff is. I run over and see my mom, lying face up in the sand. The lifeguard and a couple other people are talking, and Willa and Maya are kneeling down by her. I hear Willa laugh. My mother's eyes are open and she's smiling.

"Mom!" I say. "Jesus Christ. Mom! Can you hear me? Are you okay?"

"I'm very embarrassed," she says. She shades her eyes with the flat of her hand, blinks slowly.

"What's going on?" I say to everybody else.

"She stood up and just kind of . . . tipped over," Willa says. "Grandma, what do you feel like?"

"A bit woozy," she says. I tell the kind and curious strangers that I think we're okay—thank them for their concern, wave them away.

Now my dad is here. "Alice!" he says. "Alice!" He bends at the waist, a hand on his chest.

"I'm *alright*, Mort," she says. "Please try not to have a heart attack."

"Mort," Nick says. He pulls a chair around to my dad. "Here. Why don't you sit down."

"Help me sit up," my mother says, and I say, "Why don't you just stay lying down for another minute. Mom, did you black all the way out?"

"I don't think so," she says. I look at Willa and Maya, who both nod, mouth *yes*.

We hear approaching sirens, and the lifeguard tells us he's called an ambulance. "Oh, this is so silly," my mother says.

"I simply stood up too fast and lost my footing. Honestly. It's nothing more."

"Grandma, you really scared me," Willa says. She's smoothing my mom's hair off her face, a little tearful, and I put a hand on her back.

"I'm sorry, darling," my mother says. "I'm just a foolish old lady falling down in the sand."

"Will they take her to the hospital?" I ask the ten-year-old lifeguard, who has been talking importantly into a walkie-talkie.

"Yes," he says. "I think they pretty much have to take her to the hospital? Once you call them?"

"Way to avoid the tram line," Willa says, and my mom smiles.

I am not too distracted by the drama of my perishing mother to notice Jamie and Maya standing together, talking quietly. He's got a hand on her waist and is gazing at her, smiling, while she says something. They are such goners.

"What do you feel like, Mom?" I say, and she says, "Fine, fine. Just a little dizzy. I suppose I'm a bit warm." Her skin is actually weirdly cool, though. Clammy. "Perhaps I should drink something."

"I told you to drink something!" Willa says, because her genetic inheritance includes scolding the people you're worried about.

"I know, darling," my mother says. "I should have listened to you."

24

The fall Jamie was four and Willa was not yet one, we returned home from the Cape. Dark shapes were still sliding out of me into the toilet like poisonous sea creatures, streaming their bright, bloody tentacles behind them. "Don't come in here!" I yelled to the kids. I could hear Nick trying to lead them away from the door with raisins and toys. How had my body made so much so quickly? I knelt on the bathroom floor, reached a hand into the water, and held a clot in my palm. It was not a baby, of course, but the ache of empty arms took me completely by surprise.

25

My mother should indeed have listened to Willa. At the hospital, and pending the results of her bloodwork, they diagnose her with dehydration. They also suggest that she has some mild heat exhaustion and notice a swelling spot on her ankle, ask if she remembers being stung, if she's allergic to bees or wasps. She's doesn't; she's not.

I had traveled in the ambulance with her, during which ride she insisted she was fine before introducing herself to me and then vomiting discreetly into a vomiting receptacle that looked like a blue plastic feed bag. The EMT had started an IV with fluids but did not seem overly concerned. "She's okay," he reassured me. "Vitals are good. At her age, I'm not surprised she's disoriented." My mother's eyes had opened and narrowed into offended slits, which was actually reassuring.

Now we're in a curtained-off room in the ER, my mother asleep and snoring softly on her gurney, me seated on a small stool I've wheeled over. She is still connected to an IV, and they've added an antinausea medication to the mix, thankfully. Just because your mother is having a major health crisis doesn't mean you can really handle her barfing all over the place.

The adrenaline is wearing off a little now. I rest my forehead on the metal bars of the gurney. She is going to be okay (knock wood). But also? She is going to die. Not now (knock wood). But eventually. I mean, *obvs*, as the kids would text. But I am struck by this fact. I am stricken. Willa always says she can't spare anybody, and I'm thinking, *Me either, baby girl*. What, exactly, are we doing here? Why do we love everyone so recklessly and then break our own hearts? And they don't even break. They just swell, impossibly, with more love.

My mom always picked me up from school with a silk headscarf tied under her chin, and I'm sure I beamed with pride. *My beautiful mother!* When I sat on the edge of the tub to watch her get ready for a date with my dad, my pupils must have dilated with infatuation. She always dabbed perfume on her own wrists, and then touched one gently to the underside of my chin. I wanted to smell like her. I wanted to be her. I wanted to crawl back inside of her. Something. Everything. Instead the babysitter made Stouffer's French-bread pizza and we played Connect Four until bedtime.

When I'm jealous of my parents, I think: It was easier then. My dad worked; my mom stayed home. There was absolute clarity. Now there's just pretend equity, and it's not very romantic. Or very equitable. Nick and I both scrambled through our children's childhoods, half-assing work, half-assing home. Because I wrote from our house, I was the stay-at-home parent. Even though I earned the bulk of our income, I still had to meet the cable guy and pick up feverish kids from school and mail the holiday gifts to Florida and meet the tree guy. It was insane, and I was often furious about it. Recently, in the middle of rewatching *The Shining*, Nick said, "Oh! I'd always thought of this as supernatural horror. But it's just a movie about how scary it is to live with a writer." I have always envied my mom her loveliness. She has never seemed like a person who might axe down the kitchen door in lieu of making dinner again.

"I can't take it, Mom," I say, quietly, and she reaches out her sleeping little old-lady hand to touch my head.

I can hear before I see that everyone else has arrived now, and I go out to the waiting room to meet them. My dad is hurrying over to me, even though I've been texting them all along. "She's fine," I say to him. "She really is."

"Good," he says. "Your mother is the love of my life."

I put my arms around him. "I know that," I say into his downy white hair. "I know."

"I told you the beach was too hot," he says, "or I thought it at least and I was right." I pull away from him and say, "Dad. Let's not jump right to the blaming part. Let's linger awhile in relief and gratitude."

"Yes," he says and shakes his head. "Yes. I'm sorry. It's not anybody's fault. I'm just concerned."

"Of course," I say and catch Nick's eye. He smiles, winks at me.

"Maya and Jamie went back to the cottage," Willa says. "I promised we'd keep them in the loop."

"Great," I say. "Dad, we're allowed to go in with her one at a time. Why don't I walk you back there?"

"Please," he says. "Thank you."

Nick offers to pop out and get everyone coffee, which is a heroic idea.

I drop my dad off with the triage nurse and return to the

waiting room. There are only a handful of people here, but it's got a very ER central-casting vibe: one guy's got his elbows on his thighs, his inexpertly bandaged head in his hands; an older woman is coughing into a handkerchief while the younger woman next to her looks at her phone. I ask Willa if she wants to sit outside with me for a bit. "I could use the fresh air," I say quietly. "And also I don't really want to get pleurisy or Ebola or whatever."

We stop to buy snacks at the vending machine—Cheez-Its, a Coke, a Snickers bar—and then find a bench in the shade. We share crackers and candy, pass the soda back and forth. I try to stay vigilant because everybody's health and safety depends on it and, also, if I relax now I will fall asleep for the entire rest of my life and wake up dead. I am just happy to be sitting here in silence with this perfect human, not managing an imminent crisis. But a text dings in, and Willa says, "You should probably check that."

"It's Daddy," I say, and show her the photo he's sent of the sign at the café: *We have "ice."*

"Do you want 'ice'?" he writes, and I thumbs-up it, put the phone back in my bag. Beneath my dress, I'm still wearing a swimsuit—like the kind of person who wouldn't get a yeast infection just from imagining wearing a swimsuit all day.

"So, Maya's pregnant," Willa says.

"Oh!" I say, cagily. I know better than to be tricked into a revelation. "You're guessing or you know?"

"I know," she says. She tips her head back to dump the end of the cracker crumbs into her mouth. "I was sitting out on the deck, and I heard her and Jamie talking in the outdoor shower. I wanted to cough or something? To let them know I could hear them? But I was too curious, so I didn't. I'm the worst."

"Oh, hardly, honey," I say. "I would have done the same."

"Okay, but you're the worst too, so that's not super consoling. Anyhoo, geez, right?"

"Yeah," I say. "I already knew, to be honest."

"Yeah," she says. "I knew you knew because that's part of what they were talking about in the shower. That she'd already told you."

I cringe.

"Jamie was so cool, to be honest," she says. "I was really proud of him. He said all the right things. I felt like he did. I mean what do I know, though? Straight people are so weird. You want to get jiggy with it and then, oops, you *made a fetus*? How stupid is that? You guys are the queer ones."

"That's legit," I say, laughing. I pass her back the melting chocolate bar, and she pops the end of it in her mouth, talks to me through nougat and peanuts while I lick my fingers.

"It's so awkward, hetero sex," she says, shaking her head pityingly. "So *hydraulic*. Do you think they're going to have it?"

"I honestly don't know," I say. "Did you get a vibe?"

"Not really," she says. "Maya seemed very . . . I don't know. Rational, maybe? I couldn't hear everything even though I actually crept a little and tried to hear better, like a total creepy peepy! But she just sounded very chill."

"I admire that about her," I say, and Willa says, "Me too." Of course we do! Us, with our catastrophizing and our prescription medications. We sit quietly for a minute, listening to the chickadees in the trees. There are gulls too, salt in the air. We can't see the ocean, but I feel its massive presence.

"Did you ever get pregnant when you were that age?" Willa asks.

"I didn't," I say, truthfully. "Although it's kind of amazing, given some of the ways I used birth control. Or maybe *didn't* use birth control is a better way to describe it."

"Ew," Willa says. "I know I asked. But, just, ew. Not *you*. Just picturing you with douchey guys who were too precious to use a condom or whatever."

"Yeah," I say. "It's one of the many reasons I'm so happy you're gay."

I picture Willa and a future partner deciding, in the most deliberately loving and intentional way possible, to have a baby.

"Um, I beg to differ, because I overheard you drunkenly tell someone at Thanksgiving that you were a little *sad* I was gay because now I'd never get knocked up by accident and bring an early grandchild into your life."

"Oops!" I say. "Sorry!"

"And also, Mom? Not to be a woke pain or whatever, but it's possible I would be with a trans girl—like, a sperm-producing one—so that's probably a joke you should stop making."

"Noted," I say. "And thank you." I swallow my embarrassment.

"It's funny that *conceiving* and *conceiving* are the same word," Willa muses. "Sometimes it seems like conception is actually the opposite of having an idea."

"True," I say.

I picture a frantic montage of straight people humping nakedly against each other on the bed, on the carpet, their heads lolling around on their jack-in-the-box necks with maybe a half-empty bottle of Wild Turkey in the foreground. In the movie version, you might splice in scenes of other mating animals—rabbits, rhinos, Tom Brady, clams—everybody hump-hump-humping away with a soundtrack of circus music and creaking bedsprings. I do not share this vision with Willa.

"Did you get pregnant with me on purpose?" she asks.

"We did," I say, semi-truthfully. The whole truth is that we had intended to leave for a camping trip, but it was pouring rain, so we were stalling. We'd lumped boredly around the house until one thing led to another: Nick reaching around me to dry his hands on a dish towel; me up on the kitchen counter getting inadvertently inseminated. Nothing like *making another person* to kill a couple of minutes! Willa was conceived to the tune of the battery-operated Weebles Weebalot Castle, which Jamie was playing with in the next room.

"And then you had a miscarriage when I was little, right?" I recently learned that the kids only know this from overhearing me drunkenly tell someone at a solstice party. "Was that your only miscarriage?"

Oh! *Yes* would be the short answer.

"That's kind of a complicated question," I say instead.

"Complicated how?"

"Complicated, like, I was really sad and kind of messed up." I am flexing my calves in the air to smack my flip-flops against my heels. "It's maybe kind of a bigger story than what you want to hear."

She makes level, steady eye contact with me, and I smile. "I doubt it," she says. Those big brown eyes! I would trust this girl with my life.

But here is her father with a cardboard tray full of cold, creamy coffee, and he's been looking for us. "I think they need you back inside," he says simply. Because what else is he supposed to say?

The fall Jamie was four and Willa was not yet one, I returned to the doctor for my follow-up.

"When should I expect to get my period again?" I asked, and he said, "That depends on when your body decides to stop punishing you."

The preliminary bloodwork has come back from the lab, and the ER doc wants to talk to us about it. The Lyme test won't be done for another week or two, but everything else looks good, with the exception of my mother's total cholesterol, which is high, and something called the CRP, which might be an indicator of heart disease—and which sounds foreshadowingly to me like CPR.

To Willa too, apparently, since she says, "CPR?"

"CRP. It stands for C-reactive protein," the doctor says. If she's older than Willa, it's not by much, but she communicates an amazing combination of patience and competence.

"It's a nonspecific marker of inflammation," she says. "But we look at it to flag potential heart involvement."

My mom is sitting up now, sipping from a juice box, my dad in the chair beside her, and they both nod at this information. "Yes, yes," my mother says. "This is not news."

"Is it not?" I say, and she says, "Not really, no."

"Wait. What?"

"Mom has a bit of heart disease," my father says, like we're talking about a schmear of fucking *scallion cream cheese*!

"A bit of heart disease?" I say. I hear how shrill I sound. It is possible that I will be losing my shit.

The doctor looks at a clipboard, says, "I don't believe you indicated that to our paramedics."

"She's fine," my dad says. My dad, who was practically having his own heart attack two hours ago and is now as calm as a monk casually destroying a sand mandala.

"It hardly seemed worth mentioning," my mother says.

The doctor laughs, not unkindly. "Moving forward? It's always going to be worth mentioning."

"It's just a wonky valve," my mother says, and my father nods.

"Oh, is that all?" I say shrilly. Nick wraps an arm around my waist. A tender warning.

"She's scheduled to have it replaced," my father says, as though this should comfort me.

"Was nobody going to mention this to me?" I say.

"Of course we were, darling," my mother says. "When the time was right. I'm really fine. It's considered elective surgery, if that reassures you at all."

It actually does, to be honest.

"No," I say. "That does *not* reassure me at all. Can you please stop keeping important information from me?"

"We never would," my mother says, which is so maddening I could actually scream! Oh my god, I *am* actually screaming! No, no. I'm not. That's somebody else, in another room who has a loud something to say about needles and *keeping them the fuck away, you fuckwads*. She's probably about my age. Maybe I'm in a *Candid Camera* episode about menopause. Next thing you know my vagina will fall out onto the floor and you'll hear canned laughter.

"Sorry about that," the doctor says, tilting her head toward the profane hullabaloo. "I think, in the immediate timeframe, we're still talking about heat and dehydration. Take it easy for the rest of the day. Keep drinking water—maybe even pick up some Gatorade." My mother wrinkles her nose up at this. "We'll get in touch with your doctor at home if anything else turns up."

"Do you need to do, like, a heart thingy?" I say.

"Like a stress test or an ECG?" the doctor says, and I nod. The words "abundance of caution" float into my head, probably from George Clooney saying them on *ER* in 1994. "I don't think so. There's really nothing here that's suggestive of acute illness."

"Okay," I say. What's acute suddenly is my awareness of Willa—of Willa's awareness—and of my desire to protect her from worry, so I say, "Sounds good."

The doctor wishes us well, wishes my mother luck with the valve replacement (What the actual?), tells us we can leave at our leisure, pulls the curtain closed behind her.

"Jesus," I say. "I am very relieved and angry!"

My mother is sitting on the edge of the bed now, sorting out her clothes. "Mort, help me down," she says crisply. "I'm going to get dressed now. We'll meet you back outside."

"This week is proving to be very *revelatory*," Willa says to me in the parking lot, and I say, "Isn't it!"

28

The summer Jamie was six and Willa was not yet three, Nick said to me, "We could try again." We were in the loft bed, the kids asleep in a warm, sun-burnished tangle between us. They were so little! Their hair was so fragrant! I ached with love. It was nearing the end of our Cape week, and I felt like a gaping wound. If I could have stuffed the children into it, I would have. Into *me*. To fill the hole. To keep them safe.

To keep them.

I was crying again. "I don't think I can keep doing this," I said. It was a year after the miscarriage, and I'd been trapped on the conception roller coaster. There wasn't a better way to describe it: the rickety hope cart would creak up up up toward ovulation and then up further toward the testing period, and then—*Not pregnant!*—the cart would tip forward and zoom down through the stomach-churning descent of bloody despair, only to start its climb again immediately after. I'd really only wanted two kids, right? I didn't even know anymore. Hormones were like a hypnotist at the county fair: *You want more children!* Children! *Eyes on the swinging watch!*

All of us dazed as zombies. *More children! We want more children!*

But, then, we had friends who'd done endless, excruciating rounds of IVF—some that resulted in babies, others that didn't. My cousin's early pregnancy was interrupted with a cancer diagnosis and a hysterectomy. These were women who wanted just a single baby—who were expending their life savings and every remaining scrap of health and sanity to birth or adopt one—and we had two already. We were so lucky, by any standard! I knew that. But pregnancy loss was the hook I was hanging all my unhappiness on, and also it was the unhappiness itself. I was a human layer cake of grief and guilt, thickly frosted with shame.

People were dying to have babies. Also, people were dying not to.

I'd done so many pregnancy tests by then, half of them right in the Target bathroom, the kids crammed into the stall with me in their winter coats while the blank part of the test window stayed blank. Wait, was something turning pink? Red? Was there a second faint line? The semiotics were often baffling and always crushing, and I hallucinated positive results, dreamed about them. White sometimes looked blue. The frame around the test window cast its own small and confusing shadow that could look like a second line to the hopeful eye. There was a line of holiday shoppers out the bathroom door, miserable inside their down jackets while I monopolized a stall to squint at a stick. To trick the test, I would look away for a solid minute and then, very suddenly, look back at it. *Aha!* Nope. Nothing. "Mama! Mama! We're hot. Willa's hungry." "I know, chick. One minute." I wanted another baby in a way that obliterated my attention to the ones I already had. My greedy, irrational heart, on its knees on the tile floor, its head in its hands.

"I can't," I said to Nick. "Not again." And we didn't. But grief was like a silver locket with two faces in it. I didn't know what the faces looked like, but it was heavy around my neck, and I never took it off.

29

By the time we get back to the cottage, it's happy hour—but nobody's really that happy. We've been texting Jamie updates, and he smiles from the pull-out when we walk in, puts a finger to his lips. Maya is asleep beside him, and Chicken is curled like a massive bagel in the crook of her hip. My mother wants to lie down for a bit too—"I bet you do!" I say, like I'm accusing her of something, which I kind of am—and my father escorts her into the bedroom. I bring her an enormous glass of water and insist that she drink it while I watch.

"We're not children, Rachel," my father says coolly, and I nod.

"I know that," I say. "What do you feel like?" I ask my mom, because I am relenting.

"Just a bit tired," she says. "But I really am fine."

"Okay," I say. "Mom," I say. My eyes fill with tears. "I love you so much."

"Don't be silly," she says. "I know. Everything is fine."

"Mom," I say.

"You can't spare me," she says. "I know. You won't have

to. Not yet, at least. They're giving me a pig's valve! It's really rather exciting."

"I got confused about it because of that calamari podcast," my dad says. "The one where everyone is eating fried pig intestines and nobody can tell it's not squid."

"You thought they were making Mom a new valve out of calamari?" I say, and he says, "No. Pig bung."

"Oh, Mort, don't be revolting."

"She said it," he lies, pointing at me.

"Grandma's getting a new heart valve made out of a pork asshole," I hear Willa tell Jamie in the other room, and he says, "That's so cool!" Maya must be awake, because I hear her laughing. The hour is getting happier!

"Come have a drink with me on the deck," my dad says, as if he's reading my mind. "Your mother is never going to rest if we keep bothering her."

I look at my mom. "You're supposed to say we're not bothering you," I say, and she laughs tiredly, says, "Yes, yes. Leave me for a bit. Do."

Out on the deck, my father pours himself and Nick a glass of wine. "Me too," I say, and he says, "Aren't you drinking *that*?" and points to the two inches of dark rum I've poured into a jelly jar. I wave my hand over it. "I'm almost done with this. Just pour me some wine. Please."

The kids come out to join us, bringing seltzer and beer and chips and salsa.

"Whew," my dad says, leaning back in his chair. "What is it relief releases? In your brain? Nicotine?"

"The neurotransmitter?" Willa laughs. "I don't think it's nicotine."

"It's probably endorphins," Maya says.

"Whatever it is, whew! I'm crazy about your mother," he says to me, and I smile, say, "I know you are, Dad."

"*Grandma*," he adds, in case the kids don't know who we're talking about.

"Grandma is the best," Jamie says, then adds, "No offense, Grandpa."

My dad laughs. "None taken."

Nick puts an arm around my waist, and I realize I've barely noticed him all day. He's just here, here, here—driving us where we need to go, making everybody comfortable, cleaning up after everything, being unassumingly handsome. "Thank you," I say, close to his ear, and he squeezes me.

My dad lifts his glass in the air. "To surviving," he says, and my eyes fill with tears. "To surviving!" we all say, and clink our glasses and cans.

"If you had to walk into town," Jamie says a second later, "either completely naked or in a special suit that covered your whole body except for where there was a see-through panel in front of your crotch, which would you pick?"

This day contains multitudes. Maybe every day does.

30

The summer Jamie was four and Willa was not yet one, I did not think I could bear trying to keep another person alive. They say that having a child is like agreeing to let your heart walk around outside your body. But really your heart escapes from your body directly into the jaws of a lion. It's nothing you would ever agree to. I loved Jamie and Willa so excessively. I was so tired. I lay awake at night, and fear was the drumbeat soundtrack of my insomnia. When I heard stories about women driving themselves and their children off cliffs or into oncoming traffic, I thought, ruinedly, *Yeah. I get that.*

I wouldn't have, but I understood why you might. I *hope* I wouldn't have. I'm honestly not entirely sure.

31

Now we're on the deck, lingering over the end of our meal. Nick has gotten us clam chowder, sourdough bread, and Caesar salad from the good take-out place, and it's all delicious. Plus, the air is finally cooling off.

"Smoke show," Nick says, gesturing at the sun, which is burning low behind the clouds in glowing ribbons of pink and gray.

"Dad, that's not what *smoke show* means," Willa says, and he shrugs, but nobody has the energy to pursue it further.

My mom is a little groggy, and she's picking at her ant's portion of food, but when I visually assess her potential for imminent death, it honestly seems pretty low.

"I feel like you're not going to die, like, *tonight*," I say out loud. Oops! Am I drunk? Probably!

"Oh my god, Mom!" Willa says, but my mother laughs.

"I believe that's right," she says. "I feel fine. Truly. I'm sorry I gave everyone such a fright."

"Your mother is a resilient person," my dad says.

"You are too, Mort," Maya says, and he frowns, bobs his head side to side, like *Maybe, maybe.*

There is so much more I want to ask him. About the texture

of grief in the household of his childhood. About being a Jew. About his cranky joie de vivre. There's time, though. I mean, I hope there's time. Because this week! What on earth? And at the end of it, we'll all go our separate ways.

There are many dreadful things about the kids not living with us, but this might be the worst: returning home from vacation without them. We'll drop them at the train in Providence, and it will feel like releasing caged birds—the way they'll fly off into the station with their colorful backpacks, free. And then Nick and I will drive home with Chicken. We'll bring in the mail, unload the cooler, open the windows, feed the cat, hang the swimsuits and towels on the line. We'll leave everything else in the car and lie down in our big, empty bed so that I can cry in Nick's arms.

"You miss the kids," he'll say, pulling his face into a poor-baby frown, and I'll say, "I miss them so much."

"You loved it when they lived here."

"I loved it."

I loved it so much.

For all I know, my parents will be in their New York apartment having a similar conversation about me. It's not hard to imagine.

"Anyone want to pop into the pond?" Willa says. It's warm out, still, and there's a narrow stripe of sunset left at the bottom of the evening sky. My mother laughs, says, "No thank you, darling." Nick, Jamie, and my dad want to watch the end of the Mets game. Maya is beat. I'm beat too, but I can't resist a night swim with my daughter.

We grab towels, noodles, and, as an afterthought, suits—but

we don't bother putting them on, and we're hoping we won't need them.

Indeed, there's nobody but us at the pond. We peel off our clothes at the bench, then tiptoe over the cooling sand. The sky has darkened now, and the water looks black. I splash in quickly because I'm shy to stand out here for too long with my deflated old-lady parade-balloon body, but Willa and her gorgeous young flesh take their time.

"Tell me a snake won't slither into my vag," Willa says, and I say, "A snake won't slither into your vag." She sinks all the way down, groans in pleasure, and swims out to me with her noodle. It seems quiet at first, but the crickets and frogs make a surprising racket that gets louder the more you listen. The moon is rising over the trees. The water is cool and lovely. There's a specific smell that's like pennies and tadpoles.

"This is the best," Willa says.

"The best."

"Grandma is fine, right?" Willa says.

"Yes," I say. "She seems fine."

"Maya is okay too, I think."

"Yes, she seems okay." This girl! Doing the health-and-safety audit with me. I'm sorry she's like this, but I've never felt less alone.

"What did Dad have to say about it?"

"About what?"

"About Maya being pregnant?"

Oh, shit.

"Oh, shit," I say. "I honestly have not had a single moment to catch up with him today! I don't even know if he knows yet."

"Mom, that's terrible!" Willa scolds, and I say, "I know! It really is."

"Poor Dad! Make sure Jamie tells him."

"I will, honey. I promise."

"Don't promise that! You're crazy. What if he doesn't? You'll have broken a promise!"

"Okay, honey. I *don't* promise."

"Good."

Willa swims around a little, swims back, says, "Do you want to talk more? About what we were starting to talk about before? Your pregnancies and stuff?"

"Do you actually want to know?" I say. "I don't want you to feel obligated. You know, to be interested."

"I don't feel obligated, Mom." She tips her head back to float with the noodle under her knees. "I'm just curious. No pressure, of course."

"No, no, I want to tell you," I say. We're both gazing up at the sky now. The stars are pricking pinholes of light into the blank darkness. "I want to."

32

The summer Jamie was five and Willa was not yet two, I swallowed the pills in the car. Nick looked away, as if I might need privacy to set about disgorging our dead baby from my person. I knew exactly what to expect—the gory gynecological exorcism. The sorrow and shame. *Tell him*, I thought. *Tell him now.* But I didn't.

33

We're on our stomachs now, Willa and I, the noodles laced under our arms. The moon is illuminating the ripples we're making, light flowing out from us in concentric circles. Where they overlap they make a complicated grid pattern. I gesture to it. "You probably know the mathematical formula for this."

"The light diffraction or the capillary waves themselves? Actually, I know them both."

"Smarty," I say happily, and she says, "I'm so obnoxious! It's just that fluid dynamics is kind of my thing."

"I'm really the perfect person to brag to," I say, and she says, "True."

"There's another weird wave thing on the ocean," she says. "I don't remember what it is, only that it's called *sea clutter*."

"I love that," I say. "*Sea clutter.*"

I want to get a tattoo that says SEA CLUTTER. I want to start a band.

"So tell me," she says. "You had Jamie. You had me. Then what? Did you want to have another baby?"

"Not really," I say. "No. I mean, not at first. I really just wanted you and Jamie."

"But?"

"But I got pregnant."

"By accident?"

This is a good question. I mean, technically, yes. But also? I have never not wanted to get pregnant. Even when I was fifteen. Even, impossibly, now. I can't explain it—the way I have felt watching that wash of ink slide over a pregnancy test to catch and gather into the symbols of hope, grief, craziness. Wanting and not wanting. "That's disappointing," I learned to say, peering at a thermometer when one of my children didn't have a fever. Because, technically, you *don't* want to have a fever? But by the time someone's taking your temperature? You kind of want to have a fever.

"Kind of by accident, I guess. But it wasn't, like, a great mystery."

"Ew," she says, then laughs at herself. "Sorry! Sorry! I know you're only telling me because I'm asking. I'm the worst."

"Oh god, please," I say. "If Grandma and Grandpa were suddenly telling me this, I think I'd have to *la-la-la* with my hands over my ears."

"Okay. Then what?"

I feel the automatic urge to lie. Because I have never not lied about this. And because it's so easy. It's not even lying so much as refusing to clarify what we're talking about.

"We had a miscarriage," I say, and this is partly true. What I'm fudging now is chronological—because we did have a mis-carriage? But that was after. "Or, really, the baby died in utero, and I took the medication that makes you miscarry."

"Oh, I'm sorry, Mama. That totally sucks," she says. "Then what?"

"*Then what* what?" I say.

"Then you got pregnant again?"

"No," I say.

She treads water a little so that our eyes are level. Something is not adding up. "So you only got pregnant again the one time?"

I take a deep breath—then inhale a little water, cough and splutter, choke and stall. Willa laughs at me gently.

"No," I say, after I get my breath back. "I got pregnant another time."

"When?" she says.

"Before." A breeze sweeps over us and I shiver.

"Before Jamie?"

"No. Before the miscarriage."

"Wait," she says. "What? Oh, Mom, did you have that baby? You birthed a baby and lost it?"

"No," I say. "No, no." My throat is trying to close over the words, but I squeeze them out. "I terminated the pregnancy."

"Oh!" she says. "You had an abortion?"

"Yeah," I say. "Yes."

"This isn't the big, hard, secret thing, is it?" she says. "I mean, I'd expect you'd be cool with it."

"Not really," I say. "Which was kind of a surprise to me too. I mean, yeah, cool that I could. Cool philosophically. Politically, of course. Keep it safe, keep it legal!" I have been championing reproductive health and justice for all of my adult life. "But no. It turned out it wasn't cool for me personally. And yes, this is the big, hard, secret thing."

"How come? Oh, Mama. Are you crying?"

"Am I?" I say. "Oh, probably. It's kind of a horrible story."

A tiny head pops out of the water a couple of feet from us, and I scream. Willa screams too. We grab each other, screaming and laughing and drowning while two little googly eyes blink at us. It is not a snake. It's a turtle the size of a potato chip, and it dips back under before we can even stop screaming.

"Tell me," Willa says, breathless, once the screaming/laughing switch has been flipped back to OFF. Her eyes are huge and soft in the light of the moon. The children become the adults. It's too beautiful to bear—and too much to be worthy of. "Only if you want to, of course."

"Thank you, sweetie. I don't know. I was really overwhelmed? With motherhood. You guys were great! You were perfect. But I was so worried about you all the time. I was so ruined by my love for you. I was so tired. I couldn't imagine starting over with it. I couldn't imagine having a single extra person I was responsible for." *I never slept*, I don't say. *I watched your sleeping face and sometimes you opened your baby eyes and smiled at me and I thought I would break apart into a million pieces.*

"Were you depressed, do you think? Was it postpartum depression?" A firefly flashes above her head.

"Yeah," I say. "I think I was. I think it was. I mean, I didn't know that at the time. Because I didn't experience myself as depressed. I was just really anxious and really tired. There was always this heavy, heavy feeling of potential loss. Preemptive grief. I worried a lot that you guys would die."

"Did you wish we would so you could just get it over with?"

"Oh my god, of course not!" I say. "I mean, kind of? I know, it's so fucked up."

"No, no, I have that kind of thing too," she says. "You had an undiagnosed mental illness, Mom. It wasn't *you*."

"Thanks, honey," I say. I'm really crying now, and she swims closer to hold me in the water. She wraps one arm around my back and one under my knees like I'm a baby.

"Just a girl and her mom, bobbing in the pond," she says, which is a line from a picture book she used to love. I'm about to remind her that she's the best, the very best, when we hear a man clear his throat. I startle and flail, splash Willa, panic.

"Mom, Mom! It's okay. It's just Dad!"

"Fuck," I say, and she says, "Why *fuck*?" She pulls back to look at my face and says, "Oh my god, Mom."

34

The fall Jamie was four and Willa was not yet one, the gynecologist gave me a prescription but made me swallow the first pill in front of him like I was a child who couldn't be trusted.

"It looks like I'm going to miscarry," I said tearfully to Nick when he got home from work that evening. The tears, at least, were honest. "It may have already started."

"Oh, honey," he said. "I'm sorry." Of course! He was sorry *for me*. Because it was happening to me—this was true, whatever it was. And still the sympathy enraged me. Why were we not in this together? But we couldn't be. We weren't. Also, of course, because he didn't even know.

"You're just tired, Mama, right?" Jamie said, looking into my face with his tiny fretful eyebrows as I was tucking him in. Jesus. Had I said that to him so many times already? "I'm just tired, sweetie," I said. He patted the futon and I climbed in next to him.

"We're going to go to Cape Cod this weekend," I whispered to him, and he said, "That's so fun! Can we go to the beach? Can Willa and me get an ice cream?"

Willa had been asleep already, but she sat bolt upright like a zombie and yelled, "Ice *geem!*" Jamie and I screamed first and then laughed. And then Willa laughed too, and tackled us like a miniature lunatic linebacker, growling and shouting and laughing her maniac baby laugh directly into our faces. I drifted off with the kids piled on top of my body, anchoring me to the world.

35

Now I'm scrolling on my phone in the night. I can't sleep. I'm looking at Halloumi recipes, a root beer pound cake, someone popping corn in an open pan the size of a flying saucer. I download an alcohol-tracking app. I look at bras, acne medication, CBD vaginal suppositories. Otters floating with their pups. A guilty dog who's chewed a sofa cushion to bits. I read the Wikipedia page about Treblinka. The Wikipedia page about prolonged grief disorder. The Wikipedia page about tempeh. I watch twin babies making each other laugh. I read an illustrated wikiHow article on divorce. I imagine living alone. I could live alone! Could I? I mean, probably. *I'm definitely taking Chicken, though!* I think, defiantly.

Why do I always break my own heart?

"I heard you screaming," Nick had said from the shore once Willa and I were clambering out of the water. "I thought you'd probably seen a snake—or thought you'd seen a snake."

"Exactly," Willa said.

Nobody talked while we toweled off in the dark with a cloud of gnats buzzing around our heads. Willa went ahead of us. Nick didn't touch me on the walk back.

"The pond really carries sound, as I know you know" is all he said.

Later, we lay in bed, in the half dark, facing each other. Tears were leaking off my face into the pillow. Willa had driven off to see Callie. Everyone else was asleep, or seemed to be—but honestly who even fucking knew at this point? I practically wanted to wake them all, round them up, and tell them everything before they overheard it while they were peeing or making toast.

"Just to be clear," Nick said. "You *terminated* that first pregnancy?"

I nodded.

"And you told me it was a miscarriage?"

"Nicky."

"You pretended to be so grief-stricken."

"I wasn't pretending."

"The second one was a miscarriage or no?"

"Yes!" I said. "Of course," I added, and cringed, because why *of course*?

"You didn't feel like you could tell me," Nick said. He seemed more confused than angry. "Not then. And not now. But you were telling our daughter."

"Willa *understands* everything," I said. I was sobbing now.

Nick nodded. "It's hard to say what I would or wouldn't have understood. It's been almost twenty years, Rock. That's a lot of our marriage with a big thing in the middle of it that I didn't know." His voice caught.

"I know," I said. "I'm so sorry. I'm so ashamed."

He cupped my face, rubbed my tears away with his thumb. He was not a person who was going to yell at me or rage. I was going to be stuck hating myself instead of him. Which kind of made me hate him.

"We were in *couples therapy*," he said. "You said I didn't know you. You were furious about it. You still are. But how could I have known you, Rocky? I didn't know anything."

I wanted to say, *If you'd have wanted to know, you would have known.*

"I know," I said instead.

He must have seen it on me—the way I was cracking into fragments—because he pulled me into his chest then, held me together.

"Come here," he said, but rhetorically. I was already there. And, whether I liked it or not, he still smelled like home.

FRIDAY

36

I'm still not asleep. I try to do the thing I learned from an insomnia app: I travel through my body, turning off the light in each room. But they all flip back on behind me. I keep picking my phone up, like it's a Magic 8 Ball with answer for me. By early morning, I'm exhausted. The ceiling fan is clattering around and around, but it's hot already, and I can smell the septic. Two chipmunks chatter to each other in the tree outside our window. A mosquito is whining either outside or inside the screen—I can't tell which. Chicken is somewhere downstairs horking up a hairball, doubtless somewhere carpeted or upholstered. I hear the front door close quietly, Willa gulping water at the sink, then cursing, climbing the stairs. She flashes me a weird smile when she sees I'm awake, says, "I stepped on a fucking hairball," then gets into her little bed on the floor and rolls onto her side away from me.

I realize I don't know if my parents are still going to leave today like they've planned to. Regular people would stay at least until we have to check out tomorrow, given the whole ER situation yesterday. But my parents have a strict two-night policy. If they traveled sixty million miles to visit you on Mars, they'd bring Zabar's whitefish salad in a cooler bag and they'd stay two nights. Also, they'd complain about the traffic, the parking.

I roll over to look at Nick's sleeping face, but his eyes are open.

"Hi," he whispers.

"Hi," I whisper back. "I'm scared you're going to leave me."

He smiles. "I'm not going to leave you," he says. "I'm scared *you're* going to leave *me*!"

"I'm kind of scared about that too," I say.

His smile vanishes. "Let's try to find a time to talk. But it's okay if we can't until we get home. It can probably wait one more day at this point."

"Thank you," I say. "I appreciate that. I'm not sure what's going to be going on with everybody else today."

"Hey, do you think Maya's okay? When I went down to pee she was barfing again."

Fuuuuuuuuuck. I still haven't told him! I am a garbage bag full of secrets.

"Yeah," I say. "She's probably okay. Actually, let's really try to find a time to talk, you and me."

"Okay," he says, and kisses me chastely on the forehead. "Do you want to run with me now, before everyone gets up?"

"Oh god. Not really," I say. "I'm so tired. Do you just want to walk over to the pond, maybe? Or we could go to the ocean?"

"Sure," he says. "Either."

"Let's go to the ocean," I say, and Nick says, "Great."

We get up like groaning, kneeless stick figures, tiptoe stiffly past Willa upstairs, past Jamie and Maya downstairs, grab our damp swimsuits off the deck, pull them on in silence. There's no sound from my parents' room, and I'm glad.

Oh my god, unless they're dead! *Fuck*. I crack the door and peek in. Their lovely faces are turned toward each other, their hair white against the white pillowcases. I watch until I see the certain rise and fall of breath, then I pull the door closed again, tears in my eyes, a hand on my heart. Nick shakes his head at me, and I shrug. This is how I am, as I know he knows. When she was little, Willa used to tell ghost stories so scary she'd make herself scream and cry. I relate to the impulse.

We make coffee, drive, park. There are only a few cars this early. It's one of the wilder beaches, and we have to stagger down the steep, sandy dune to get to it. The kids used to fly down this hill, tumbling at least as often as they stayed on their feet. They held out elbows, chins. *Kiss this, Mama. And here.* So many scrapes and bruises! So many consoling handfuls of Goldfish crackers!

"Walk?" Nick says. "Sit?"

"Sit with me," I say.

The tide is going out, and the sand is cool and damp as we near the water. We sit on our towels. I fuss with mine a little, spread it out around me, stall. A seagull flying low overhead drops something into the sand near us and swoops down to grab it up, giving us an indignant side-eye.

"We weren't going to steal your crab," I say. "Geez."

Nick is lying back, balanced on his forearms, and he turns his handsome face to me. "It was your decision to make," he says. "Always. Obviously."

"I know," I say. I'm already crying, wiping at my face with the sleeve of Nick's one nice shirt, which I'm wearing un-buttoned over my suit.

"Did you think I was going to pressure you to have it?"

"No. No. Not really. But I don't think this is the right conversation to have. You're going to be barking up this rational tree, and I'm going to be alone in a different tree, not getting barked at."

He looks puzzled, which is reasonable. I sigh, try again.

"You're probably studying it from all these angles, like, *Does this make sense? Does* this? But it's not going to be clear like that, the reason I didn't tell you." He's looking at the water, but I feel his attentiveness.

"Nick, you know, like, one thousand awesome philosophical arguments for abortion rights, and I love you for that. I agree with all of them. Obviously." Before he went to school to become a physical therapist, Nick got a PhD and taught ethics to college students.

"But it's not like that. I didn't think it was unethical—of course—not in that way. But I felt terrible about it, about myself. I was too in love with the babies we had to have another baby. I was so wrecked, Nicky. I didn't have a reason I could explain to you. I can't even explain it now."

He nods uncertainly.

"And then, afterwards, I was so sad. I was too in love with the babies to survive the fact that we weren't having another one—that I'd chosen not to. And I just wanted to get pregnant again. It was a kind of possession. That pregnancy had set something in motion, and the only exorcism was going to be pregnancy. I was desperate about it. I was so sorry. So regretful. The moment I swallowed that pill! I would have given anything to get it back. Almost anything." I knew the due date—what the baby's birthday would have been. And then, after the miscarriage, I knew that baby's birthday too. I still mark these anniversaries. Am marked by them. "Nick, I was just accruing all these losses, and the whole time I was still so worried about Jamie and Willa. That something would happen to them. That we had everything to lose." The year after my last pregnancy, my friend Jo was rear-ended and her car was trashed. An insurance claim was opened in the Department of Total Loss. "Same," I said when she told me, and she said, "What?" and I said, "Department of Total Loss," and then, "Nothing," because I knew I wasn't making any sense.

Nick sits up now. He puts a hand on my back. "Oh, honey," he says, and I tip over into him.

"This is a lot," he says, wiping his chest with the edge of his towel, "of snot."

I honk out a weird phlegmy laugh.

"So who knew?" he asks, and I sit up again, shake my head. The water is swelling and breaking, churning up pebbles. It sounds like someone is shaking an enormous jar of dried beans. The moon does all this? It's hard to fathom.

Nick is looking at me, waiting. "Nobody," I say.

"You didn't tell *anybody*?"

"Right."

"Not even Jo?"

"Not even Jo."

"The therapist you were seeing then?"

I shake my head again.

"You didn't tell your *therapist*?"

"I was worried she was going to pathologize me," I say, and then laugh. "Which was kind of pathological, I realize."

"Wowza, honey," Nick says.

"It got so much better once I started taking an antidepressant. I think the miscarriage made me feel like I could finally ask for help. But an abortion? That's kind of a bed you have to lie in. I mean, it shouldn't be. It's not. I would try to argue anybody else out of that feeling. But that's how I felt."

I peel off the shirt now, pull my hair up off the back of my neck.

"Hot flash," I say. Nick looks alarmed—and for good reason. "But I've been so mad at you. Yes, for not knowing. For not seeing me. For not seeing more. But also for being so fucking *whole*. So unscathed."

Nick nods nervously.

"It's, like, total reproductive mayhem every second. A gynecological shit show. And then I'm supposed to be excited about sex? Like we're riding a Ferris wheel in a fucking cemetery! It's *insane*."

Nick chews his thumbnail. But I have more to say!

"We're just ruined by sex, women—our bodies, our psyches. We're sexually assaulted every five minutes. We're infected with everything. Traumatized by conceiving, by not conceiving. But let's keep at it! Like, you've been in a maiming car accident and then you're supposed to want to get back in the car? I mean, what?"

"But people do," Nick says. "Get back in the car."

"Yeah," I say. "But there's no expectation that you're going to, like, have multiple orgasms on the highway in the middle of your trauma flashback."

"You know you want me," Nick says to make me laugh, and I do. I do laugh. I do want him.

"I actually do want you," I say. "But sometimes I feel like

we're living on two different planets. And then I remember that that's the name of that stupid book—the Venus and Mars one—and I'm so mad I could scream."

"Do you want to go in?" Nick says, gesturing at the water. *Let's get you a handful of Goldfish crackers!* But yes, I want to. I want to swim. I want to feel tugged. And I want to feel weightless.

37

As Nick's pulling in at the cottage, I remember.

"Shit!" I say. "Fuck. There's something else."

"Uh-oh!" Nick says. He's driving barefoot and bare-chested, like a teenager.

"Honey. Maya's pregnant."

"Oh!" Nick says. He nods. "Wow. Okay. What's the plan?"

"I don't know," I say. "I don't think they know."

"Wow. When did they tell you?"

"Yesterday," I say. Nick waits for me to say more, but I'm busy tugging the swimsuit out of my crack. "Maya told me. Wait. What day is it? No. Not yesterday. The day before yesterday, I think?" I tip my head back to drink the end of a cup of coffee that turns out to definitely not be from today. Nick is looking straight ahead, but I see his mouth pulled into a flat line.

"Oh no! You're making your small face. Are your feelings hurt? I'm sorry! I'm so sorry. I didn't mean to not tell you. I was waiting until she told Jamie, and then the day kind of got away from me."

"It's okay," he says. He laughs grimly. "I don't imagine the main thing going on right now is that I'm a little offended. I just feel kind of out of the loop in general."

And it boils up in me. "Jesus, Nick. I mean, you don't want it—you actively do not want to be the person people talk to about their feelings. But then you're hurt when they don't. And that leaves me to do it, like it always fucking has. Can you turn on the car so I can open my window? It's broiling."

Nick twists the key, rolls all the windows down, turns to face me.

"Someone has to be the person who drives everyone every-where and gets dinner and isn't swept away in everybody's drama every second, Rock." That's fair.

"That's not fair," I say. "I do all the emotional work."

"True. But some of it is work of your own making. I don't really know that you need to be at the center of some of the things you're at the center of."

"Oh my god. You're calling me a narcissist?"

"A little bit, yeah."

"I really am kind of a narcissist, tbh."

Nick laughs. "I know."

"But you suck, Nicky! You look away from anything you don't want to see."

"That's true," he says. "I know you do so much. I really do know that."

"But are you going to apologize for being a pain in my ass?" I say, and he says, "I don't think so, no. I don't feel an apology of that breadth coming on."

"A smaller apology, then?"

He puts a finger on his chin, considering. "Not at this time, no."

I shake my head, half furious, half besotted. Truly both things.

I climb into his lap, straddle him awkwardly with one knee wedged into a cupholder, lean down to kiss him. I pull back to look at him. "You sure have a lot of pretty teeth," he says, smiling, then wraps his hands around my hips. There are only swimsuits between us, only heat. I push forward and he groans. And, yes, despite the full reproductive catastrophe of my life, despite the dry fury of menopause, I have depended on Nick for this—for groaning. For wanting me. I have craved it all my life. I vow for the millionth time to be more wifely. Prettier, nicer. What the fuck, though? Why should I have to be pretty and nice? Why the actual fuck? But his hands are in my hair, his mouth on my neck, and I am so, so lucky.

He presses up into me, hard, and whispers, "You're going to be a hot grandma," and I say *Oh my god* because our baby is having a baby.

Maybe.

38

Everybody is awake. The couch is made back up, and Willa and Maya are sitting together with the cat and mugs of coffee, looking at a *Gourmet* magazine from 1985. "They were very, very excited about their chicken with olives and prunes and a full quarter-cup of dried oregano," Willa announces.

My dad is out on the deck with the newspaper. Jamie and my mom are making bacon and pancakes. "Did you buy a newspaper for Grandpa?" I ask Jamie, and he says, "I did!" "You're a good child," I say, and he says, "I try." I lean in to greet my alive mom, and she tips her jaw toward me for a kiss.

I gather plates and silverware, carry everything out to the deck. Nick follows me with glasses and juice, opens the umbrella over the table, though it's still shady back here for now. The air is pine-scented and filled with birdsong.

"Good morning," my dad says, and I say, "Hi, Dad! Did you guys sleep okay?"

"Your cat knocked over my water glass," he says.

"I'm so sorry, Dad! He's a bad cat."

"Relatedly," he says. "I forgot and flushed a paper towel, which I know you're not supposed to do."

"I'm sure it's fine," I lie.

Willa comes out with the maple syrup and a container of cut-up watermelon. Jamie, Maya, and my mom appear with the rest of the food.

"How is it Friday already?" I say, and everybody laughs because wowza—it has been a week and a half! We pass the food around in silence for a minute, pass the syrup, fill water glasses, juice glasses.

"You're really fine, Grandma?" Willa says, and my mom says, "Right as rain."

"Drink a little more, okay?" Willa says, and my mom nods, drains her water glass obediently.

"But you're not going to drive home today, are you?" I say. The pancakes are tender and a little bit tangy. Did someone get buttermilk? "These are delicious, by the way," I say.

"Of course we are," my mother says. "We'll leave after breakfast. Your father's going to drive." My father never drives.

"You're okay to drive, Dad?"

"Why wouldn't I be okay to drive?" My dad is rolling up two pieces of bacon in a pancake, dipping it in a pool of syrup.

"Um, because you're three hundred years old, Grandpa," Willa says, and he chuckles.

"I'm a pretty good driver still," he says, which is not true. But at least he's never been a good driver.

"Mort, let me drive you guys," Nick says. "I can just take the train back up. I love the train!"

Nick might as well have offered to zip my dad into his footie pajamas. My father holds an offended finger in the air while he chews and swallows. "That won't be necessary, Nicholas," he says.

"Will you guys please wear your masks if you stop at that huge rest area?" Willa says. "I really don't want you to get Covid." Even for Willa, I don't imagine my parents are about to put masks on.

"I think I finally got Covid recently," my dad says, and I say, "What?" *Stop* is what I want to say. *Stop not telling me things.* Or maybe *Stop telling me things.*

My mother shakes her head. "I don't know, Mort. I'm not convinced."

"Well, I am," my dad says. "I boiled an egg one morning last week and it was very plain-tasting."

We all look at him, waiting for more, so he says, "It tasted fine after I salted it, though."

"That was the extent of your symptoms, Dad?" I say. "A plain-tasting egg?"

"Yes," he says.

"Oh my god, Grandpa," Willa says, laughing.

"Yes, Willa?" he says, and she says, "Nothing. I'm just glad you recovered."

Jamie interrupts. "Before you go," he says, "Maya and I have something we want to share with you all." I see him catch her eye, and she smiles her dazzling smile at him. Nick squeezes my hand. I'm going to be a hot grandma!

"Sorry to be so dramatic," Jamie says, grinning. "I mean, now you already know what I'm going to say. Maya and I are getting married!" *Oh! Okay.* I inhale deeply so that I won't react to the wrong thing. These precious children.

My mother claps and says, "Yay!" and my father congratulates them. Nick and I stand to walk around the table, put our arms around them, tell them we love them.

"I'm so excited for you!" Willa says. "Good job, you guys! It's going to be so much fun. I want to be the best man. Or whatever the thing is that's not me in a dress and where I get to bring a cute girl."

"Those might be two different things," Maya says. "But you can definitely do both of them."

"Let me see your ring," my mother says, and then, "Oh, of course not, silly me!" when they tell her they haven't gotten a ring—that it was just a spontaneous decision they made together.

"Do you have a date in mind?" I ask.

"Maybe next summer?" Jamie says. "After Maya's course-work is done."

"Great!" I say. They'll have a four-month-old! I can hold the baby during the ceremony. I'm glad they're not rushing to wed before Maya starts showing. "You can do it on the Cape!" I say. "Or in our yard at home!"

"I think we might do it at Maya's parents' house in New Jersey," Jamie says shyly, and I blush, say, "Of course!" There are other people in the world besides us! I forget sometimes.

"But that's such a nice offer, Rocky," Maya says. "Thank you."

"Oh, of course. Sorry to be weird. Have you told your parents yet?"

"We called them earlier this morning," Jamie says. Already with the *we*! I make a mental note to rearrange my heart—to make a little more room for the changing realities. But geez! *What about us?* I want to say. *Don't we matter at all?*

. . .

And then I remember that they're here with us, right now, telling us everything.

While we're clearing the table, I hear my mother offer to mend Maya's shorts. She's brought a sewing kit, she says. "Oh," Maya says, and laughs. "These are kind of meant to be ripped up like this."

"How peculiar!" my mother says. "I don't always understand the world anymore."

"Me either, Ma," I say, and lean against her without, amazingly, toppling her to the ground.

39

Good-bye! Good-bye! We all wave as my parents drive off. We all dash over after my dad backs the Volvo into a shrub, wave again after it turns out to be fine. *Good-bye! Good-bye!*

"Jesus," I say, and collapse against Nick. He kisses the top of my head.

"I always worry when they leave that I'll never see them again," Willa says and bursts into tears.

I fold her into my arms and say, "I know what you mean, honey," because anticipatory grief is among the top five worst traits she's inherited from me. It might even be in the top three. "I learned to be like this from *you*," she says, the angry little mind reader, and I say, "I know. I'm really sorry."

"Do you think it's epigenetic trauma?" she asks as we walk back into the cottage. "Epigenetics is when something that happens during your own lifetime becomes inheritable?" I say, and she says, "Basically."

"It might be," I say. "I don't totally understand how that works. I know there's a lot of trauma in our family, though. Obviously more than I even realized."

She nods. "I want to do a load of laundry before I go back," she says. "Keep me company?" Of course!

Willa gathers up her dirty clothes, which are scattered so widely around the loft that it's like they erupted from a butch volcano.

"Why are your socks in our bed?" I ask her, and she shrugs. Chicken hops into her open suitcase in his poignant gambit to not be left behind. Willa pretends not to see him, zips him inside, and he's crouched down, as excited and wide-eyed as a little child when she unzips it again. "There you are!" she says. "I was looking everywhere!" He flops onto his back to show us his creamy tummy, purring. Then he gathers himself into a confusing tangle of paws and feet. Poor old Chicken.

"I miss you so much when you're at college," I say in Chicken's voice, and Willa says, "Oh, you poor boy."

In the laundry building, Willa dumps her paper bag of clothes into a washing machine and I toss in some towels, glug in detergent, fit quarters into slots, and pick a setting. Willa presses START and sits in a folding chair, pats the chair next to her.

"Here?" I say, and she shrugs.

"Just for a minute. It's the only place nobody else will be." This is true.

"Did you get to talk to Dad?" she asks.

"I did."

"Was it okay?" God, *was* it?

"Which thing?" I say.

"Either," she says. "Both."

"I think so," I say. "I'm embarrassed that you're spending your whole vacation worrying about me."

She waves her hand dismissively. "I'm not. Why didn't you tell him before?" she asks. "Was it someone else's baby?"

"Oh god! No. That would really be a big secret, though!" I say. "It was nothing like that. I just—I felt a lot of shame about it."

"About having an abortion?"

"Kind of. About not wanting to have the baby."

"There's nothing shameful," she says. "You shouldn't have felt shame about that."

"Well, don't *shame* shame me," I say, and she smiles, nods.

"It's not abortion in the abstract," I say. "It was mine. My specific experience. My body. My weird mental state. My fear. And then I regretted it so much."

"Mom!" She's horrified. "You can't regret an abortion! That's such a dangerous thing to say. The religious right will, like, eat that shit up."

"Willa, honey. It's just us in a laundromat. I'm not running for governor."

"Still," she says. "I don't think you should have felt regret."

"But I did. I'm just a person. That's part of choice—we get to make our own decisions, even if they're imperfect. The potential that you might regret something? We don't make anything illegal because of that. You regretted dating that impossible girl in high school."

"Angelina," Willa says, and shudders.

"Angelina," I say. "She was the worst! But we don't ban gayness just because you might make a poor gay choice."

She laughs. "True. We don't ban straight-people marriage either, even though mostly people get divorced."

"True," I say back. "Or, like, Jamie had that horrible

internship—he regretted taking it. But we don't legislate against getting a job."

"If only!" Willa says.

"I wish that it would have been great for me. That I would have terminated the pregnancy and felt relief, lightness. Lots of people I know have had that experience, and I'm so happy for them. I want that for everybody! But I didn't. And that's okay. I survived it. But it was hard."

"If you didn't want to have a baby, why did you get pregnant again, after the abortion?"

"Well, then I *did* want to have another baby. After not having the other one."

"Like, *atonement*?"

"No, no. Not like that. More like an antidote to sadness."

"Mom, are you less pro-choice than I thought you were?"

"Oh my god, no!" I say. "Willa, I have literally risked my life for women's access to abortion."

"Trans men too," she says, and I say, "Trans men too."

"And nonbinary people."

"And nonbinary people," I say.

"Drama queen, though," she says. "I mean, *you risked your life*? Mom. Please."

"Um, yeah, I think I kind of actually did. Back when I used to be an escort at the clinic. I think I actually risked my life."

She nods. "Okay," she says. "Rad."

"You will never need to terminate a pregnancy," I say smugly. "I love that about your life."

"Mom!" she says. "That's crazy. I mean, good job being woke about my gayness, etcetera. But yes, of course I might need to terminate a pregnancy. If I didn't want to be pregnant or a pregnancy was going wrong or if something happened to the baby."

"Yes," I say. "Sorry. That was a stupid thing to say. Do you picture being pregnant?"

"I don't," she says. I put a hand over her hand to stop her from picking at a scab on her shin, and she shakes me off. "If I had to guess, I'd guess I won't? But I have no idea how I'll feel later—and when I see pregnant queers or pregnant trans men it definitely makes me excited about the world. But that's different from wanting to be pregnant. I want to have a partner who wants to be pregnant, though."

Good, I think. But I don't trust myself to say anything that won't annoy her.

A woman comes in with a laundry basket under one arm, a crying little girl under the other.

"Sorry," she says, and I say, "Oh my god, please. Can we help?"

"No," she says, "thanks," and plops the girl down onto the floor, where she rolls onto her back, crying and kicking the floor with her little flip-flops.

"It was mine," she is crying.

"Yes." The mom is sorting laundry into two machines. "That was your shell. But that shell was still being used by a snail. That was a stinky shell and we put it back in the pond."

"That was *my* stinky shell!" the girl is crying.

"That shell was too stinky," the mom says, shutting the machines.

"I wanted it was stinky!" the girl cries. "I liked it was stinky!"

"You can play with the shells at the pond, but we can't take them home," the mom says.

The girl is kicking and crying, and her mom looks at me, pulls her face into an exaggerated silent scream.

"I've been there," I say, and she says, "Thanks."

"I like stinky shells too," Willa says. The girl rolls onto her side on the concrete floor to eyeball my ungirly daughter. She herself is wearing pink swimsuit bottoms and a tiny little pink T-shirt that says BEACH BUM in silver glitter. "I always want to keep the stinky shells and nobody ever lets me." This is completely true.

"Me too!" the girl says, shocked, as if Willa has divined this similarity out of thin air.

"It's the worst," Willa says. The girl pops her thumb into her mouth, grabs a handful of her own hair in the other hand, sucks and nods.

She pulls her thumb out of her mouth to say, "I miss my shell. I miss my stinky snail in it."

"I know how you feel," Willa says.

And this may be the only reason we were put on this earth. To say to each other, *I know how you feel*. To say, *Same*. To say, *I understand how hard it is to be a parent, a kid*. To say, *Your shell stank and you're sad. I've been there*.

40

There are wounds that never really heal, no matter how much time they take.

Jamie and Willa were both born by C-section, and for years afterward the scar would reopen randomly, rupture like a fault line. I didn't care. It reminded me of the luck of it—of having the kids. Of birthing them safely. But boy, my body kept the score. When Willa was fifteen—and I know you can do the math, but yes, this was *fifteen years* after that second C-section—a pimple formed on my belly, near the scar. A cyst, maybe. And it got bigger and bigger and then burst, like a malevolent life-form from one of the *Aliens* movies. What emerged was a knotted piece of suturing. I pulled it out with tweezers and it was so gross that I couldn't get anybody to look at it. "Bear witness!" I said, approaching the kids with the tweezers. "I am still recovering from your births, *motherfuckers!*" But they shrieked and ran away and refused to look.

There was no bodily evidence of the pregnancies that came after. They left no visible scars. But these were the wounds I thought I might never recover from. I'm not sure even now if I have or will. What does loss look like, in your body? Where is it? It feels like an air bubble stuck in your psyche. It feels like peering down into a deep hole. The vertigo of that. The potential for obliteration. It's in your stomach. Your spleen.

Or it's just your heart losing its mind.

41

Back in the cottage, all the windows are wide open, and a breeze is blowing through, bringing with it the pink smell of phlox and roses. I'm sad and relieved about my parents leaving. I'm furious with and crazy about Nick. I'm remorseful. Grateful. I'm excited for Maya and Jamie, and worried about them. I am amazed by Willa. I am drowning in love. My great-grandparents were murdered by Nazis. The world is achingly beautiful. I am fifty-four years old, and I know better, finally, than to think you have to pick. That you even could. It's just *everything, all the time. EVERYTHING.* Put it on my tombstone! *EVERYTHING!*

"Everything?" Nick says. The train in my brain between thinking and speaking has really gone off the rails.

"Everything," I say, and he smiles nervously at me, the way he often does.

"The last day!" Jamie says. "What are we doing?"

"I mean—beach, right?" I say, and everybody agrees. I open the fridge. "We've got nine eggs we need to use up. I'll make egg salad. What do people want in their egg-salad sandwiches?"

"Hmm," Jamie says. "I don't think I really want egg salad."

"Me either, tbh," Willa says.

"Oh, okay. Do you want to do, like, a room-temp fried-egg sandwich?" I am very flexible!

"Let's pick up sandwiches from the deli," Jamie says.

"These eggs, though."

"We can just bring them home tomorrow," Nick says.

I'm standing with the carton of eggs in my hand, shocked right to my sandwich-making core.

"Or throw them away," Jamie says, laughing. "I mean, not to be all Bill Gates about this. But seriously, Mom. It's eggs."

I drop the carton directly into the very full trash, but just to make everybody laugh—which they do—before I yoink it out and return it to the fridge.

"Okay! We'll buy lunch."

"Oh my god, is she offended?" Willa says. "Mom!"

"Am I? Maybe I am. That's dumb, though. Especially since I can get that gross seafood salad I love, the one with the fake crab in it. I'm in! I'm down. This is good."

And it is good. Jamie places our order online, from the car, so it's ready by the time we get there. Five sandwiches in a brown paper bag with five black-and-white cookies, five bottles of iced tea.

"This was an excellent idea!" I say and mean it. "Eggs are for losers."

Back in the car, squashed between Maya and me, Willa says, "I always picture it like pickled sausages, pressed up against the glass. Her nose and lips and stuff."

"Um," Jamie says from the passenger seat. "Say more?"

"Eleanor Rigby's face. In a jar by the door." She sings the line from the Beatles song. "Also, Maya, you might know the answer to this. But when a caterpillar—what's the verb form of it?—*metamorphosizes*, what happens to its brain? Like, does every other part of it get melted down to make a butterfly, but its little brain just stays intact the whole time?"

"Most of the brain tissue gets broken down and rebuilt," Maya says. "I mean, it makes sense, right? It has to be a pretty significant neurological rearrangement to get a brain to send *fly* signals instead of *crawl* signals."

"Wow" is all Willa says, but I am thinking of these people in the car with me. These no-longer-kids, who have emerged from the cocoon of childhood to fly away into the wild, so brilliant and beautiful. Whose brains have liquefied and re-arranged themselves to pilot this flight.

It's been so hard, the kids leaving home. In their absence, I have scanned the world for traces of them, like a lovestruck detective. Jamie doesn't post on Instagram, but his friends sometimes tag him. One weekend, when he was housesitting for my parents, I saw photos of a party he was throwing in their apartment. I zoomed in on the marble coffee table where there was a bong— a bong *on a coaster*—and I screenshotted it, sent it to him. "A coaster!" I wrote. "Good boy." He sent me the crying-laughing emoji. They're too cheap to get their own Amazon Prime accounts, the kids, so they use ours still, for the free shipping. I get a Venmo notification and the "Your Amazon.com order has shipped" email and click to see what they've purchased, try to piece together the lives lived without me: Jamie has bought twelve cat-ear headbands; Willa has bought a coloring book; Jamie has bought a luxury hair product, kitchen sponges, and a package of four Bic lighters in "fashion colors"; Willa has bought Taylor Swift temporary tattoos and *The Handbook of Developmental Cognitive Neuroscience*; Jamie has bought a stain-removal pen; Willa has bought a *Controlling Your Anxiety* interactive workbook, the same luxury hair product as Jamie, and a supplement called L-theanine. I fret about them; I make notes to myself about how best to fill their Christmas stockings.

I'm on a Facebook group for parents of semi-grown kids, and everyone is the same, all of us lost in the fog, mooing out our worry to the other lost cows. Most of the time, the moms are worried about drugs, and they post anxious photos of evidence found in their children's backpacks and dressers: "Does anyone know what this is?" they write, assuming the worst in a drug-paraphernalia sense. "That's spray Neosporin," someone reassures. "Those are Necco wafers." "Tire-pressure gauge." "Playmobil chicken leg." We don't know what we're seeing or what it means. *Is my kid okay?* is all anybody is really asking. *I miss them*, we say. *What am I supposed to do next?*

When Willa left for college I said to Nick, "Well, silver lining, we can start eating meat again!" For a silver lining it was pretty bleak, and we didn't even do it. I cried, I was bereft, and we kept eating beans and tofu. There were more rooms in the house to fight or have sex in, and we could fight or have sex more noisily and to no end. This was a mixed bag.

You hear the expression *empty nest* and imagine the downy expanse of it, the absence of cheeping, maybe the bird pair connecting more intimately, what with nobody barging in at midnight needing either of them to read an email to their history teacher or inspect a weird freckle that turns out to be Magic Marker. But often an empty nest is two birds looking at each other, shell-shocked and nostalgic, over the single worm they're now splitting for dinner, discussing what to do with the worm leftovers.

My own parents have been doing this for years, making food for just themselves, and it always makes me laugh. "I got a lovely piece of halibut from Whole Foods," my mother will tell me, before describing its many iterations throughout the week: on Monday, my mother broiled the fish and served it with buttered new potatoes; on Tuesday, my dad mixed the leftover fish and potatoes with cooked barley, sautéed mushrooms, and little grape tomatoes; on Wednesday, they ate the remaining halibut-barley combo over noodles; on Thursday, everything that was left went into a casserole with two beaten eggs and some chopped dill. "You guys!" I say. "Please try not to give yourselves botulism." "Well, at least we're not like Grandma," my dad says about his own mother, who would famously have added various cycles of freezing and thawing to this choreography of orts.

As it turned out, I had been essentially hosting Jamie and Willa for decades—throwing a permanent kind of dinner party that I wanted the kids to never want to leave. The food was good, the entertainment varied; we loved them well, and now they're gone.

You're supposed to retrace your steps when you lose something, but none of my losses are like that. Where would I look for them? And what would I do if I found them? Little ghost babies, born babies, outgrown children's bodies, missing teenagers. Loss like a shipwreck. Swim down to it, down, down, down to the pitch-black ocean floor, where nothing is visible and it never dissolves.

. . .

"Is it actually pitch-black on the ocean floor?" I ask Maya now, in the car, and she says distractedly, "In the abyssopelagic zone, it is."

"Obvs," I say, and she laughs. WELCOME TO THE ABYSSOPE-LAGIC ZONE! The sign nobody ever sees.

We do the sequence of things—parking lot, tram, walkway, beach—and here we are, scanning for a break in the density of human bodies and stuff, spotting a free patch, and staggering over to dump everything into the sand. Nick immediately pulls off his Red Sox T-shirt and Red Sox cap and asks Willa if she wants to swim with him. "Nah," she says. "I'm lazy. I'm just going to lay in the sun for a while." Nick catches my eye because *lay* instead of *lie*, but we don't say anything because we're trying not to be colonialist grammar-police fucktrumpets or whatever it is Willa has accused us of being. Jamie and Maya are already out walking along the shoreline. They have a lot to discuss, I'm sure. Or maybe they don't. What do I know?

"I'll go!" I say, and Nick reaches out a hand for me.

At the waterline, though, I get a sudden case of the goose bumps and chicken out. Nick waits while I stall. While I squat down to look at a piece of sea glass, a pretty stone.

"Did you just put a pebble in your mouth?" he says, and I say, "No."

"Rocky."

"I'm not going to swallow it! I just wanted to feel how smooth it was. It's so salty! Here." I spit it out, smile.

"Catch me if you can!" I say, like we're suddenly in a romantic comedy, and I run through the froth to dive under the waves, with Nick so close behind he grabs me before I'm in too deep.

42

But it's really not like a romantic comedy, and here's how I know: Two minutes later, we're fighting again.

"There's so much to process," I yell to Nick in the cold froth of the breaking waves, and he says, "Yeah."

"What do you feel like?" I say, and he shrugs. "Are you feeling *anything*?" I say, and he knows it's a trick question. "No," he says, and he laughs, but I don't.

"*Actually* no?" We're jumping up as each wave threatens to break over us, shouting to hear each other over the roar of the surf. The water is achingly cold and so salty my eyes are burning.

I can't hear Nick sigh, but I know he does. He shakes his head, pushes his dripping hair off his face with a weary palm, jumps up and twists away from me to avoid another wave. We are at the edge of an unfathomable ocean, eighty-two billion *billion* gallons of brine sloshing away from us toward Portugal. I am an insignificant speck—just over a single gallon of blood pumping around in this piece of bony, fatty human luggage—picking a fight with a man who wants to ride the waves into shore and clamber out happily to eat his boughten sandwich.

Here's what foragers know: Most of what grows is neither delicious nor toxic. There's a whole world between what we call the choice edibles—the hazelnuts and porcini and black raspberries—and, say, the destroying angel mushroom that will shut down all your organ systems after a single nibble. You can eat the grass, the lichen, the inner bark of most trees, a thousand kinds of leaves. Not that you would, but you could. So much of privileged adulthood seems to take place here, in the space between the soaring highs and the killing disasters. It's just plain life, beautiful in its familiar subtlety, its decency and dailiness. Nick is never going to sing me a climactic aria. I will not be scoured clean by his anger and forgiveness. It's up to me now, to unravel this rope I've twisted together from shame and guilt and rage and sadness.

"You could decide to be happy," a friend told me once. She's a therapist, and we were walking in the woods near my house, stopping every now and then to call back to an owl who was hooting at us from the trees. "The rest of it? Put it in a little boat in your mind and just push it out to sea." "Are you telling me to repress my sorrow and anger?" I said, surprised, and she said, "Not repress. *Set free*." "I have to think about that," I said.

I'm thinking of it now even as a wave is crashing over me. I tumble around in sand and salt, find my hands and knees, and crawl toward solid ground. *Leave it*, I think to myself, like I'm a dog with something in its jaws: a squirrel, a frankfurter, a pair of underpants, a grief habit. *Leave it.*

43

Willa once shared her theory that finding a four-leaf clover was a symptom of luck, not a cause. "It just means you have the kind of life where there are growing things and you have time to look at them," she said. I think she was actually making a point about class privilege? But I like to imagine that luck is everywhere, even before you find it.

On the way back to the cottage from our last beach day, we stop for ice cream. It's so tempting to waste the last of the time we have left in a state of preemptive loss that I have to actively stop myself from the ruing and keening. "You guys are so tall!" is what I hear myself say instead, and the kids do not dignify this with a response—they just look at me like I'm a batty old fool because I am and because they stopped growing years ago. *How are these adults my children?* is what I really want to say. *And why are they so beautiful?* Willa, with her shoulders and cheekbones and her darkly shorn, perfectly shaped head. Jamie, with a manly shadow along his lovely jaw, above his lovely lips. I've heard grief described as *love with nowhere to go.* To be honest, though, I sometimes feel like love is that already. All I can do is wrap an arm around Nick's waist and lean in to get a consoling kiss on the head.

In line in front of us, one boy says to another, "Just plain vanilla? You can't get that. Vanilla is so gay."

"I mean, he's not wrong," Willa says. She and Nick are always trying to figure out what the chocolate flavor is that's going to be the very chocolatiest. They ask questions about ripples, chunk size, and darkness. Me? I just want a kiddie-sized vanilla soft-serve cone because that's how gay I am, even though this provokes a pitying head shake from the chocolate snobs. Maya gets cotton candy, which Nick and Willa some-how approve of, and Jamie gets black raspberry, which they don't.

We carry our dripping cones over to a picnic table beneath the pines to discuss our favorite moments of the week. Nick's is lobster. Jamie's is lobster too, and mini-golf, and also a vague and unelaborated entry, which is *family*, and which appears to be spoken for my benefit. ("Aw, honey," I say obligingly.) Maya's is arranging a rainbow out of the subtly colored stones on the beach and also finding a perfectly intact knobbed whelk shell with a shiny pink inside. "Oh, also getting engaged!" she tacks on, and Jamie laughs, says, "Same!" Willa's is hermit crabs and night swimming and when my mother was telling us about her new pharmacist named Regina—with a long *i*. Willa and Jamie had caught each other's eye and keeled over into the sand with laughter. "Honestly," my mother had scolded them, and they tried to pull themselves together but couldn't. "Your children," my mother had scolded me, and I'd said, "I know," but I was pressing a towel against my mouth to stop myself from laugh-ing too.

"Remember that summer you baked a lemon cake in a litter pan?" Willa says now. She's already laughing again, biting at the end of her cone and pressing a napkin against the corners of her eyes.

"I didn't bake a cake in a litter pan," I say.

"Did you or did you not bake a cake in a pan that had had cat litter in it?"

"It had cat litter in it for, like, a minute—just while I was dealing with the real litter pan. It was that summer Chicken was sick. It was a disposable aluminum pan and I washed it really well and threw it out after."

"Threw it out after what?"

"After baking a cake in it," I concede.

The kids fall against each other laughing.

Have you pictured Daedalus watching from his own great height as the wings of his son started to come loose, pulled away by heat and gravity? Have you seen, in churches and museums, the enormous body of Jesus draped across his mother's lap? I know you know about Sandy Hook. About police violence, war, illness, genocide, famine, terror. There are so many ways to lose our children, and I have imagined most of them—imagined the near ecstasy of it, the violins sawing out grief's unfathomable song.

Nobody has asked me what my favorite part of the week is, but maybe that's because they know I'll say, boringly, that it's simply this: the fact of us together and alive. The kids are doubled over still with the hilarity of it all. They are so grown! So young. Mine and not mine, as ever they have been. Maybe grief is love imploding. Or maybe it's love expanding. I don't know. I just know you can't create loss to preempt loss because it doesn't work that way. So you might as well love as much as you can. And as recklessly. Like it's your last resort, because it is.

"Should we pack up a little before dinner?" Nick says, and everybody groans. "Let's go to the pond instead," Willa says. "Before we run out of time." So that's what we do.

After

Now we're accompanying Jamie and Maya down the aisle in her parents' backyard. All of us, with Maya's brothers and sisters and parents too, a brimming, boisterous crowd handing these gorgeous batons off to each other 'til death do them part.

I've always hated euphemisms about the end of life. *Just say* dead *or* died*!* I've wanted to say, crankily, when a phrase enters my ears about that person passing on, passing away, leaving us too soon. But I think I was wrong. A transition is so much gentler than an ending—and in a million ways, my mother is here with us still. In our photographs and our memories. In our hearts and even our lungs because she is the air we breathe.

When she was in hospice, her heart failing quickly while ours beat on and on, we watched the birds outside her window. The kids came and went, loving and devastated, but also busy with work and school. My mom dozed while my dad read the paper and I mended my jeans. Sometimes she was in pain, and it was awful. Sometimes I looked at take-out menus with my dad and she grinned at us from her weird bed. Her strength and coordination failed, and I climbed in next to her to help with her phone, using her thumb to unlock the screen like it was a tool in my own hands. "I'm still a person!" she said, indignant, as I repeatedly jabbed her thumb on the button. We laughed so much I cried and then peed a little, and then we laughed about that too: her continent on her deathbed; me borrowing a pair of her underpants.

"Stupid useless calamari heart valve," I said, lightly thumping her sternum one night.

She pishposhed and said, "I must tell you something." My dad had left the room to make her a piece of cinnamon toast. *Oh no*, I thought. *Don't tell me.* I felt almost phobic about divulgences. "Tell me," I said bravely, and what she told me was that I didn't need to draw so many conclusions, to make so many decisions. That I could just live with all the different parts of a life as they were. That I could be happy even though nothing would ever be perfect. And this was so close to what I'd already been thinking myself that it astonished me. "Thank you," I said, and she nodded.

"Love will be the death of me," I said.

"Sweetheart, no. *Death* will be the death of you." This seemed inarguably true.

"Are you scared?" I asked.

"I'm not," she said, and didn't seem to be. "Death is no more than passing from one room into another." *Into another room where all the dead people are*, I didn't say. "Helen Keller," she added, by way of attribution, and then she swished her hand in the air because now she was done with this kind of talk and wanted me to brush her beautiful hair before my dad got back.

She waited to die until I left the room, which is a thing I've heard parents do. I can imagine it. I mean, you're never done being somebody's mom, ever, are you? She took care of me until the very end.

We spread some of her ashes in Central Park, where the daffodils first come up in April. "Imagine trying to make that color yellow just from the soil and sunlight," Willa said. She was leaning against my father, who was smiling and frowning and dabbing at his face with a handkerchief. "Like, if someone was like, here's a bowl of dirt. Make two perfect shades of the brightest yellow you ever saw! You totally couldn't do it." We agreed that this was true. "So what is that? I mean, I know it's nature. Photosynthesis. Adaptation. But is it magic too?" We thought that maybe it was.

I've written down one stanza of the Emily Dickinson poem "After great pain, a formal feeling comes" and tacked it over my desk.

> This is the Hour of Lead—
> Remembered, if outlived,
> As Freezing persons, recollect the Snow—
> First—Chill—then Stupor—then the letting go—

"Yikes!" Nick said. "So, like, *freeze to death*?"

"No! No. Like, *let go of your pain*." The ghost babies visited only occasionally now, and they never cried.

"I don't know," Nick said, and I didn't know either. And, yes, somehow that was okay.

I found a deli receipt with the sentence *How alive your heart to feel such sorrow!* written on the back in my handwriting. Where was it from? I googled it, got zero results. Did I write it in my sleep? I pinned it up next to the poem.

Also, we got a rescue kitten—what Willa called "our overlap cat," in case Chicken dies, and she's not wrong. The kitten's tag said PRECIOUS when we got her, so that's her name. She has bright green eyes and a weirdly small head, and Chicken is so overwhelmed with affection that he heaves his enormous bulk on top of her and purrs and you wouldn't even know she was under there. He's like a roosting hen. "You're so precious to me, Precious," Willa says in Chicken's voice, and Precious says, from beneath him, "You're precious to me too."

"Don't keep secrets from each other," Willa will say, when she toasts the bride and groom an hour from now. There's no baby. Jamie will have his arm around Maya's shoulders, both of them beaming like a two-strobe lighthouse. *The beams of love.* "You can, like, close the bathroom door"—everyone will laugh—"and keep your old journals to yourselves. But share everything that matters. And keep loving each other massively. Life's too short for anything else." The room will erupt, and I will lean into Nick, happy and sad. Broken and healing. My dad will twist in his chair to smile at me. I will smile back. We'll be missing my mom. We'll be tending our wounds.

And we'll be as young and as whole as we're ever going to be.

Acknowledgments

My wonderful editor, Sara Nelson, makes me feel normal and funny and good, and this is such a gift to me that I hardly know how to thank her except by saying thank you, Sara. Many thanks also to Edie Astley, for her excellent eye and sense of things. And to Maya Baran and Katie O'Callaghan, thank you again, in advance, but also thank you in arrears (?) for selling my last book so passionately and well. Dear copy editor Janet Rosenberg, thank you for your care and patience. Virginia Stanley, enthusiastic lover of books, writers, and libraries, thank you for your huge heart. And everyone else at Harper who does so much and so well: Ahhhhh, you're the best.

Thank you, as always, to Jennifer Gates, who is so lovely and gracious that you might hardly notice that she's brilliantly busy getting you the sun and the moon. Thank you also to the amazing Erin Files and Allison Warren, who conceal neither their enthusiasm nor their talent, and to everyone else at Aevitas who is doing the work so well.

Thank you, dear readers! The readers of this book, you, thank you! And also the readers of my last book, including the librarians, booksellers, book reviewers, blurbers, bookstagrammers, book clubs, podcasters, interviewers, and listeners. Special thanks to Michael Millner, Becky Michaels, and Kathleen Traphagen, who read this manuscript early and lovingly and led me to imagine it could be an actual book. Birdy Newman also read an early version and gave me such useful and beautiful feedback that I cried through my first round of edits.

Very specific gratitude to: the lovely Joanna Goddard, who let me write about empty nesting for Cup of Jo; Karen E. Bender and Nina de Gramont for their anthology *Choice*, where I first wrote about reproductive mayhem; Jennifer Niesslein, who always encouraged me to write my angriest, craziest shit; Sandra Tsing Loh, the "absolute legend" referenced at the Ladies' Library book sale; Shoshana Marchand for "stroke clinic;" and Emily Franklin for the DM.

My friends sustain me daily: my mom friends, family friends, Amherst College friends, Fisher Home friends, weird friends, writing friends, work friends, polar-plunge friends, Zumba friends, social media friends, young-people friends, and my oldest friends in the world, here and gone. You all know who you are. Special shout-outs to the small but hugely essential Amherst Tire Running Club, to constant rain-or-shine companion Maddie DelVicario, and to Lydia Elison, who slips me therapy when I'm just bent over to look for four-leaf clovers.

I love my brother, Robert; his wife, Alba; and the four boys: Sam, Lucas, Andreu, and Max. I love my niblings and cousins and aunts and uncles, and also my many, many in-laws, including and especially Fan Club President Larry Millner. I'd be bored and lonely without the pussycats Snapper and Jellyfish.

I need to praise Michael Millner not just for being the most patient, loving, fun-loving, and sexily gray-templed person on

025

the planet, but also for being so expansively generous about my writing, even when you'd think all of it might be kind of awkward. Thank you, my love.

It is a great privilege to be sandwiched between my beautiful, wonderful, hilarious parents, Ted and Jennifer Newman, and my beautiful, wonderful, hilarious children, Ben and Birdy Newman. I couldn't love any of you more than I do, but I probably will anyway.

About the Author

CATHERINE NEWMAN has written numerous columns, articles, and canned-bean recipes for magazines and newspapers, and her essays have been widely anthologized. She is the author of the novel *We All Want Impossible Things*; the memoirs *Waiting for Birdy* and *Catastrophic Happiness*; the middle-grade novel *One Mixed-Up Night*; and the bestselling kids' life-skills books *How to Be a Person* and *What Can I Say?* She lives in Amherst, Massachusetts.